WALT WHITMAN'S
Short Stories

New-York.
1848.

Copyright © 1841-48 Walt Whitman
Spelling, punctuation, and grammar from original magazines.

public domain
www.chollaneedles.com

ISBN: 172451296X
ISBN-13: 978-1724512963

CONTENTS.

Death In The School Room	1
Wild Frank's Return	6
The Child's Champion	12
Bervance: or, Father and Son	21
The Tomb-Blossoms	29
The Last of the Sacred Army	35
The Child-Ghost	40
Reuben's Last Wish	48
A Legend of Life and Love	53
The Angel of Tears	57
The Reformed	61
Lingave's Temptation	64
The Madman	68
The Love of the Four Students	72
Eris; A Spirit Record	78
My Boys and Girls	81
The Fireman's Dream	84
Dumb Kate - An Early Death	92
The Little Sleighers	95
The Child and the Profligate	98
Shirval: A Tale of Jerusalem	108
Richard Parker's Widow	112
The Boy-Lover	117
The Death of Wind-Foot	123
Revenge and Requital	129
Some Fact-Romances	139
The Shadow and the Light of a Young Man's Soul	145

Short Stories.

DEATH IN THE SCHOOL-ROOM.

A FACT.

TING-A-LING-LING-LING!—went the little bell on the teacher's desk of a village-school one morning, when the studies of the earlier part of the day were about half completed. It was well understood that this was a command for silence and attention; and when these had been obtained, the master spoke. He was a low thick-set man, and his name was Lugare.

"Boys," said he, "I have had a complaint entered, that last night some of you were stealing fruit from Mr. Nichols's garden. I rather think I know the thief. Tim Barker, step up here, sir."

The one to whom he spoke came forward. He was a slight, fair-looking boy of about fourteen; and his face had a laughing, good-humored expression, which even the charge now preferred against him, and the stern tone and threatening look of the teacher, had not entirely dissipated. The countenance of the boy, however, was too unearthly fair for health; it had, notwithstanding its fleshy, cheerful look, a singular cast as if some inward disease, and that a fearful one, were seated within. As the stripling stood before that place of judgment, that place, so often made the scene of heartless and coarse brutality, of timid innocence confused, helpless childhood outraged, and gentle feelings crushed—Lugare looked on him with a frown which plainly told that he felt in no very pleasant mood. Happily a worthier and more philosophical system is proving to men that schools can be better governed, than by lashes and tears and sighs. We are waxing toward that consummation when one of the old-fashioned schoolmasters, with his cowhide, his heavy birch-rod, and his many ingenious methods of child-torture, will be gazed upon as a scorned memento of an ignorant, cruel, and exploded doctrine. May propitious gales speed that day!

"Were you by Mr. Nichols's garden-fence last night?" said Lugare.

"Yes, sir," answered the boy: "I was."

"Well, sir, I'm glad to find you so ready with your confession. And so you thought you could do a little robbing, and enjoy yourself in a manner you ought to be ashamed to own, without being punished, did you?"

"I have not been robbing," replied the boy quickly. His face was suffused, whether with resentment or fright, it was difficult to tell. "And I didn't do anything last night, that I'm ashamed to own."

"No impudence!" exclaimed the teacher, passionately, as he grasped a long and heavy ratan: "give me none of your sharp speeches, or I'll thrash you till you beg like a dog."

The youngster's face paled a little; his lip quivered, but he did not speak.

"And pray, sir," continued Lugare, as the outward signs of wrath disappeared from his features; "what were you about the garden for? Perhaps you only received the plunder, and had an accomplice to do the more dangerous part of the job?"

"I went that way because it is on my road home. I was there again afterward to meet an acquaintance; and—and— But I did not go into the garden, nor take anything away from it. I would not steal,—hardly to save myself from starving."

"You had better have stuck to that last evening. You were seen, Tim Barker, to come from under Mr. Nichols's garden-fence, a little after nine o'clock, with a bag full of something or other, over your shoulders. The bag had every appearance of being filled with fruit, and this morning the melon-beds are found to have been completely cleared. Now, sir, what was there in that bag?"

Like fire itself glowed the face of the detected lad. He spoke not a word. All the school had their eyes directed at him. The perspiration ran down his white forehead like rain-drops.

"Speak, sir!" exclaimed Lugare, with a loud strike of his ratan on the desk.

The boy looked as though he would faint. But the unmerciful teacher, confident of having brought to light a criminal, and exulting in the idea of the severe chastisement he should now be justified in inflicting, kept working himself up to a still greater and greater degree of passion. In the meantime, the child seemed hardly to know what to do with himself. His tongue cleaved to the roof of his mouth. Either he was very much frightened, or he was actually unwell.

"Speak, I say!" again thundered Lugare; and his hand, grasping his ratan, towered above his head in a very significant manner.

"I hardly can, sir," said the poor fellow faintly. His voice was husky and thick. "I will tell you some—some other time. Please to let me go to my seat—I a'n't well."

"Oh yes; that's very likely;" and Mr. Lugare bulged out his nose and cheeks with contempt. "Do you think to make me believe your lies? I've found you out, sir, plainly enough; and I am satisfied that you are as precious a little villain as there is in the State. But I will postpone settling with you for an hour yet. I shall then call you up again; and if you don't tell the whole truth then, I will give you something that'll make you remember Mr. Nichols's melons for many a month to come:—go to your seat."

Glad enough of the ungracious permission, and answering not a sound, the child crept tremblingly to his bench. He felt very strangely, dizzily—more as if he was in a dream than in real life; and laying his arms on his desk, bowed down his face between them. The pupils turned to their accustomed studies, for during the reign of Lugare in the village-school, they had been so used to scenes of violence and severe chastisement, that such things made but little interruption in the tenor of their way.

Now, while the intervening hour is passing, we will clear up the mystery of the bag, and of young Barker being under the garden-fence on the preceding night. The boy's mother was a widow, and they both had to live in the very narrowest limits. His father had died when he was six years old, and little Tim was left a sickly emaciated infant whom no one expected to live many months. To the surprise of all, however, the poor child kept alive, and seemed to recover his health, as he certainly did his size and good looks. This was owing to the kind offices of an eminent physician who had a country-seat in the neighborhood, and who had been interested in the widow's little family. Tim, the physician said, might possibly outgrow his disease; but everything was uncertain. It was a mysterious and baffling malady; and it would not be wonderful if he should in some moment of apparent health be suddenly taken away. The poor widow was at first in a continual state of uneasiness; but several years had now passed, and none of the impending evils had fallen upon the boy's head. His mother seemed to feel confident that he would live, and be a help and an honor to her old age; and the two struggled on together, mutually happy in each other, and enduring much of poverty and discomfort without repining, each for the other's sake.

Tim's pleasant disposition had made him many friends in the village, and among the rest a young farmer named Jones, who with his elder brother, worked a large farm in the neighborhood on shares. Jones very frequently made Tim a present of a bag of potatoes or corn, or some garden vegetables, which he took from his own stock; but as his partner was a parsimonious, high-tempered man, and had often said that Tim was an idle fellow, and ought not to be helped because he did not work, Jones generally made his gifts in such a manner that no one knew anything about them, except himself and the grateful objects of his kindness. It might be, too, that the widow was loath to have it understood by the neighbors that she received food from any one; for there is often an excusable pride in people of her condition which makes them shrink from being considered as objects of "charity" as they would from the severest pains. On the night in question, Tim had been told that Jones would send them a bag of potatoes, and the place at which they were to be waiting for him was fixed at Mr. Nichols's garden-fence. It was this bag that Tim had been seen staggering under, and which caused the unlucky boy to be accused and convicted by his teacher as a thief. That teacher was one little fitted for his important and responsible office. Hasty to decide, and inflexibly severe, he was the terror of the little world he ruled so despotically. Punishment he seemed to delight in. Knowing little of those sweet fountains which in children's breasts ever open quickly at the call of gentleness and kind words, he was feared by all for his sternness, and loved by none. I would that he were an isolated instance in his profession.

The hour of grace had drawn to its close, and the time approached at which it was usual for Lugare to give his school a joyfully-received dismission. Now and then one of the scholars would direct a furtive glance at Tim, sometimes in pity, sometimes in indifference or inquiry. They knew that he would have no mercy shown him, and though most of them loved him, whipping was too common there to exact much sympathy. Every inquiring glance, however, remained unsatisfied, for at the end of the hour, Tim remained with his face completely hidden, and his head bowed in his arms, precisely as he had leaned himself when he first went to his seat. Lugare looked at the boy occasionally with a scowl which seemed to bode vengeance for his sullenness. At length the last class had been heard, and the last lesson recited, and Lugare seated himself behind his desk on the platform, with his longest and stoutest ratan before him.

"Now, Barker," he said, "we'll settle that little business of yours. Just step up here."

Tim did not move. The school-room was as still as the grave. Not a sound was to be heard, except occasionally a long-drawn breath.

"Mind me, sir, or it will be the worse for you. Step up here, and take off your jacket!"

The boy did not stir any more than if he had been of wood. Lugare shook with passion. He sat still a minute, as if considering the best way to wreak his vengeance. That minute, passed in death-like silence, was a fearful one to some of the children, for their faces whitened with fright. It seemed, as it slowly dropped away, like the minute which precedes the climax of an exquisitely-performed tragedy, when some mighty master of the histrionic art is treading the stage, and you and the multitude around you are waiting, with stretched nerves and suspended breath, in expectation of the terrible catastrophe.

"Tim is asleep, sir," at length said one of the boys who sat near him.

Lugare, at this intelligence, allowed his features to relax from their expression of savage anger into a smile, but that smile looked more malignant, if possible, than his former scowls. It might be that he felt amused at the horror depicted on the faces of those about him; or it might be that he was gloating in pleasure on the way in which he intended to wake the poor little slumberer.

"Asleep! are you, my young gentleman!" said he; "let us see if we can't find something to tickle your eyes open. There's nothing like making the best of a bad case, boys. Tim, here, is determined not to be worried in his mind about a little flogging, for the thought of it can't even keep the little scoundrel awake."

Lugare smiled again as he made the last observation. He grasped his ratan firmly, and descended from his seat. With light and stealthy steps he crossed the room, and stood by the unlucky sleeper. The boy was still as unconscious of his impending punishment as ever. He might be dreaming some golden dream of youth and pleasure; perhaps he was far away in the world of fancy, seeing scenes, and feeling delights, which cold reality never can bestow. Lugare lifted his ratan high over his head, and with the true and expert aim which he had acquired by long practice, brought it down on Tim's back with a force and whacking sound which seemed sufficient to awake a freezing man in his last lethargy. Quick and fast, blow followed blow. Without waiting to see the effect of the first cut, the brutal wretch plied his instrument of torture first on one side of the boy's back, and then on the other, and only stopped at the end of two or three minutes from very weariness. But still Tim showed no signs of motion; and as Lugare, provoked at his torpidity, jerked away one of the child's arms, on which he had been leaning over the desk, his head dropped down on the board with a dull sound, and his face lay turned up and exposed to view. When Lugare saw it, he stood like one transfixed by a basilisk. His countenance turned to a leaden whiteness; the ratan dropped from his grasp; and his eyes, stretched wide open, glared as at some monstrous spectacle of horror and death. The sweat started in great globules seemingly from every pore in his face; his skinny lips contracted, and showed his teeth; and when he at length stretched forth his arm, and with the end of one of his fingers touched the child's cheek, each limb quivered like the tongue of a snake; and his strength seemed as though it would momentarily fail him. The boy was dead. He had probably been so for some time, for his eyes were turned up, and his body was quite cold. The widow was now childless too. Death was in the school-room, and Lugare had been flogging A CORPSE.

———

WILD FRANK'S RETURN.

The main incidents of this and another story, "Death in the School-Room," contributed by the same writer to a preceding number of the Democratic Review, were of actual occurrence; and in the native town of the author, the relation of them often beguiles the farmer's winter-fireside.

    As the sun, one August day some fifty years ago, had just passed the meridian of a country-town in the eastern section of Long Island, a single traveller came up to the quaint, low-roofed village-tavern, opened its half-door, and entered the common room. Dust covered the clothes of the wayfarer, and his brow was moist with sweat. He trod with a lagging, weary pace; though his form and features told of an age not more than nineteen or twenty years. Over one shoulder was slung a sailor's jacket, and in his hand he carried a little bundle. Sitting down on a rude bench, he told a female who made her appearance behind the bar, that he would have a glass of brandy and sugar. He took off the liquor at a draught; after which he lit and began to smoke a cigar, with which he supplied himself from his pocket—stretching out one leg, and leaning his elbow down on the bench, in the attitude of a man who takes an indolent lounge.
    "Do you know one Richard Hall that lives somewhere here among you?" said he.
    "Mr. Hall's is down the lane that turns off by that big locust-tree," answered the woman, pointing to the direction through the open door; "it's about half a mile from here to his house."
    The youth, for a minute or two, puffed the smoke from his mouth very leisurely in silence. His manner had an air of vacant self-sufficiency, rather strange in one of so few years.
    "I wish to see Mr. Hall," he said, at length. "Here's a silver sixpence for anyone who'll carry a message to him."
    "The boys are all away.—It's but a short walk, and your limbs are young," replied the female, who was not altogether pleased with the easy way of making himself at home, which marked her shabby-looking customer.
    That individual, however, seemed to give small attention to the hint, but leaned and puffed his cigar-smoke as leisurely as before.
    "Unless," continued the woman, catching a second glance at the sixpence; "unless old Joe is at the stable, as he's very likely to be. I'll go and find out for you." And she pushed open a door at her back, stepping through an adjoining room into a yard, whence her voice was the next moment heard calling the person she had mentioned, in accents by no means remarkable for their melody or softness.

Her search was successful. She soon returned with him who was to act as messenger—a little, withered, ragged old man, a hanger-on there, whose unshaven face told plainly enough the story of his intemperate habits—those deeply-seated habits, now too late to be uprooted—that would ere long lay him in a drunkard's grave. The young man informed him what the required service was, and promised him the reward as soon as he should return.

"Tell Richard Hall that I'm going on to his father's house this afternoon. If he asks who it is that wishes him here, say the person sent no name," said the stranger, sitting up from his indolent posture, as the feet of old Joe were about leaving the door-stone, and his bleared eyes turned to catch the last sentence of the mandate.

"And yet, perhaps you may as well," added the youth, communing a moment with himself: "you may tell him his brother Frank, Wild Frank, it is, who wishes him to come." The old man departed on his errand, and he who called himself Wild Frank tossed his nearly smoked cigar out of the window, and folded his arms in thought.

No better place than this, probably, will occur to give a brief account of some former events in the life of the young stranger resting and waiting at the village inn. Fifteen miles east of that inn lived a farmer named Hall, a man of good repute, well off in the world, and head of a large family. He was fond of gain—required all his boys to labor in proportion to their age,—and his right-hand man, if he might not be called favorite, was his eldest son Richard. This eldest son, an industrious, sober-faced young fellow, was invested by his father with the powers of second in command; and as strict and swift obedience was a prime tenet in the farmer's domestic government, the children all quietly submitted to their brother's sway—all but one, and that was Frank. The farmer's wife was a quiet woman, in rather tender health; and though for all her offspring she had a mother's love, Frank's kiss ever seemed sweetest to her lips. She loved him more than the rest—perhaps, as in a hundred similar instances, for his being so often at fault, and so often blamed. In truth, however, he seldom received more blame than he deserved, for he was a capricious, high-tempered lad, and up to all kinds of mischief. From these traits, he was known in the neighborhood by the name of Wild Frank.

Among the farmer's stock there was a fine young blood mare—a beautiful creature, large and graceful, with eyes like dark-hued jewels, and her color that of the deep night. It being a custom of the farmer to let each of his boys have something about the farm that they could call their own, and take care of as such, Black Nell, for so the mare was called, had somehow or other fallen to Frank's share. He was very proud of her, and thought as much of her comfort as his own. The elder brother, however, saw fit to claim for himself, and several times to exercise a privilege of managing and using Black Nell, notwithstanding what Frank considered his prerogative. On one of these occasions a hot dispute arose, and after much angry blood, it was referred to the farmer for settlement. He decided in favor of Richard, and added a harsh lecture to his other son. The farmer was really unjust; and Wild Frank's face paled with rage and mortification. That furious temper which he had never been taught to curb, now swelled like an overflowing torrent. With difficulty restraining the exhibition of his passions, as soon as he got by himself he swore that not another sun should roll by and find him under that roof. In the night he silently rose, and, turning his back on what he thought an inhospitable home, in mood in which child should never leave the parental roof, bent his steps toward the city.

It may well be imagined that alarm and grief pervaded the whole of the family, on discovering Frank's departure. And as week after week melted away and brought no tidings of him, his poor mother's heart grew wearier and wearier. She spoke not much, but was evidently sick in spirit. Nearly two years had elapsed, when about a week before the incidents at the commencement of this story, the farmer's family were joyfully surprised by receiving a letter from the long absent son. He had been to sea, and was then in New-York, at which port his vessel had just arrived. He wrote in a gay strain; appeared to have lost the angry feeling which caused his flight from home; and said he heard in the city that Richard had married, and settled several miles from home, where he wished him all good luck and happiness. Wild Frank wound up his letter by promising, as soon as he could get through the imperative business of his ship, to pay a visit to his home and native place. On Tuesday of the succeeding week, he said, he would be with them.

Within half an hour after the departure of Old Joe, the form of that ancient personage was seen slowly wheeling round the locust-tree at the end of the lane, accompanied by a stout young man in primitive homespun apparel. The meeting between Wild Frank and his brother Richard was hardly of that kind which generally takes place between persons so closely related; neither could it be called distant or cool. Richard pressed his brother to go with him to the farm-house, and refresh and repose himself for some hours at least, but Frank declined.

"They will all expect me at home this afternoon," he said, "I wrote to them I would be there to-day."

"But you must be very tired, Frank," rejoined the other; "won't you let some of us harness up and carry you? Or if you like—" he stopped a moment, and a trifling suffusion spread over his face; "if you like, I'll put the saddle on Black Nell—she's here at my place now, and you can ride home like a lord."

Frank's face colored a little, too. He paused for a moment in thought—he was really foot-sore, and exhausted with his journey that hot day,—so he accepted his brother's offer.

"You know the speed of Nell as well as I," said Richard; "I'll warrant when I bring her here you'll say she's in as good order as ever." So telling him to amuse himself for a few minutes as well as he could, Richard left the tavern.

Could it be that Black Nell knew her old master? She neighed, and rubbed her nose on his shoulder; and as he put his foot in the stirrup and rose on her back, it was evident that they were both highly pleased with their meeting. Bidding his brother farewell, and not forgetting Old Joe, the young man set forth on his journey for his father's house. As he left the village behind, and came upon the long, monotonous road before him, his mind began to meditate on the reception he should meet with. He thought on the circumstances of his leaving home; and he thought, too, on his course of life, how it was being frittered away and lost. Very gentle influences came over Wild Frank's mind then, for he yearned to show his parents that he was sorry for the trouble he had cost them. He blamed himself for his former follies, and even felt remorse that he had not acted more kindly to Richard and gone to his house. Oh, it had been a sad mistake of the farmer that he did not teach his children to love one another. It was a foolish thing that he prided himself on, of governing his little flock well, when sweet affection, gentle forbearance, and brotherly faith, were almost unknown among them.

The day was now advanced, though the heat poured down with a strength little less oppressive than at noon. Frank had accomplished the greater part of his journey; he was within three miles of his home. The road here led over a high, tiresome hill, and he determined to stop on the top of it and rest himself, as well as give the animal he rode a few minutes' breath. How well he knew the place! And that mighty oak, standing just outside the fence on the very summit of the hill, often had he reposed under its shade. It would be pleasant for a few minutes to stretch his limbs there again as of old, he thought to himself; and he dismounted from the saddle and led Black Nell under the tree. Mindful of the comfort of his favorite, he took from his little bundle, which he had strapped behind him on the mare's back, a piece of small, strong cord, four or five yards in length, which he tied to the bridle, and wound and tied the other end, for security, round his own wrist; then throwing himself at full length upon the ground, Black Nell was at liberty to graze around him, without danger of straying away.

It was a calm scene, and a pleasant. There was no rude sound—hardly even a chirping insect—to break the sleepy silence of the place. The atmosphere had a dim, hazy cast, and was impregnated with overpowering heat. The young man lay there minute after minute, as time glided away unnoticed; for he was very tired, and his repose was sweet to him. Occasionally he raised himself and cast a listless look at the distant landscape, veiled as it was by the slight mist. At length his repose was without such interruptions. His eyes closed, and though at first they opened languidly again at intervals, after a while they shut altogether. Could it be that he slept? It was so, indeed. Yielding to the drowsy influences about him, and to his prolonged weariness, he had fallen into a deep, sound slumber. Thus he lay; and Black Nell, the original cause of his departure from his home—by a singular fatality the companion of his return—quietly cropped the grass at his side.

An hour nearly passed away, and yet the young man slept on. The light and heat were not glaring now: a change had come over the aspect of the scene. There were signs of one of those sudden thunder-storms that in our climate spring up and pass over so quickly and so terribly. Masses of vapor loomed up in the horizon, and a dark shadow settled on the woods and fields. The leaves of the great oak rustled together over the youth's head. Clouds flitted swiftly in the sky, like bodies of armed men coming up to battle at the call of their leader's trumpet. A thick rain-drop fell now and then, while occasionally hoarse mutterings of thunder sounded in the distance: yet the slumberer was not aroused. Lo! thus in the world you may see men steeped in lethargy while a mightier tempest gathers over them. Even as the floods are about to burst—as the warning caution is sent forth, they close their eyes, and dream idly, and smile while they dream. Many a throned potentate, many a proud king with his golden crown, will start wildly in the midst of the thundercrash, and the bright glaring of the storm, and wonder that he saw it not when it was coming.

It was strange that the young man did not awake. Perhaps his ocean-life had taught him to rest undisturbed amid the jarring of elements. The storm was now coming on in its fury. Black Nell had ceased grazing, and stood by her sleeping master with ears erect, and her long mane and tail waving in the wind. It seemed quite dark, so heavy were the clouds. The blast came sweepingly, the lightning flashed, and the rain fell in torrents. Crash after crash of thunder seemed to shake the solid earth. And Black Nell, she stood now, an image of beautiful terror, with her fore feet thrust out, her neck arched, and her eyes glittering balls of fear. At length, after a dazzling and lurid glare, there came a peal—a deafening crash—as if the great axle was rent; it seemed to shiver the very central foundations, and every object appeared reeling like a drunken man. God of Spirits! the startled mare sprang off like a ship in an ocean-storm—her eyes were blinded with terror—she dashed madly down the hill, and plunge after plunge,—far, far away—swift as an arrow,—dragging the hapless body of the sleeper behind her.

In the low, old-fashioned dwelling of the farmer there was a large family group. The men and boys had gathered under shelter at the approach of the storm; and the subject of their talk was the return of the long absent son. The mother spoke of him, too, and her eyes brightened with pleasure as she spoke. She made all the little domestic preparations—cooked his favorite dishes—and arranged for him his own bed, in its own old place. As the tempest was at its fury they discussed the probability of his getting soaked by it; and the provident dame had already selected some dry garments for a change. But the rain was soon over, and nature smiled again in her invigorated beauty. The sun shone out as it was dipping in the west. Drops sparkled on the leaf-tips,—coolness and clearness were in the air.

The clattering of a horse's hoofs came to the ears of those who were gathered there. It was on the other side of the house that the wagon road led; and they opened the door and rushed through the adjoining room to the porch. What a sight it was that met them there! Black Nell stood a few feet from the door, with her neck crouched down; she drew her breath long and deep, and vapor rose from every part of her reeking body. And with eyes starting from their sockets, and mouths agape in stupifying terror, they beheld on the ground near her a mangled, hideous mass—the rough semblance of a human form—all battered, and cut, and bloody. Attached to it was the fatal cord, dabbled over with gore. Fearful and sickening was the object. And as the mother gazed—for she could not withdraw her eyes—and the appalling truth came upon her mind, she sank down without shriek or utterance, into a deep, deathly swoon.

THE CHILD'S CHAMPION.

JUST after sunset one evening in summer—that pleasant hour when the air is balmy, the light loses its glare, and all around is imbued with soothing quiet—on the door-step of a house there sat an elderly woman waiting the arrival of her son. The house was in a straggling village some fifty miles from the great city, whose spires and ceaseless clang rise up, where the Hudson pours forth its waters. She who sat on the door-step was a widow; her neat white cap covered locks of gray, and her dress though clean, was patched and exceeding homely. Her house, for the tenement she occupied was her own, was very little, and very old. Trees clustered around it so thickly as almost to hide its color—that blackish gray color which belongs to old wooden houses that have never been painted; and to get to it, you had to enter a little rickety gate, and walk through a short path, bordered by carrot-beds, and beets, and other vegetables. The son whom she was expecting was her only child. About a year before, he had been bound apprentice to a rich farmer in the place, and after finishing his daily tasks, he was in the habit of spending half an hour at his mother's. On the present occasion, the shadows of the night had settled heavily before the youth made his appearance; when he did, his walk was slow and dragging, and all his motions were languid, as if from great weariness. He opened the gate, came through the path, and sat down by his mother in silence.

"You are sullen, to-night, Charley," said the widow, after a minute's pause, when she found that he returned no answer to her greetings. As she spoke, she put her hand fondly on his head; it was as wet as if it had been dipped in the water. His shirt, too, was soaked; and as she passed her fingers down his shoulder, she felt a sharp twinge in her heart, for she knew that moisture to be the hard wrung sweat of severe toil, exacted from her young child, (he was but twelve years old,) by an unyielding task-master.

"You have worked hard to-day, my son."

"I've been mowing."

The widow's heartfelt another pang. "Not all day, Charley?" she said in a low voice, and there was a slight quiver in it.

"Yes, mother, all day," replied the boy; "Mr. Ellis said he couldn't afford to hire men, for wages is so high. I've swung the scythe ever since an hour before sunrise. Feel of my hands." There were blisters on them like great lumps.

Tears started in the widow's eyes. She dared not trust herself with a reply, though her heart was bursting with the thought that she could not better his condition. There was no earthly means of support on which she had dependence enough to encourage her child in the wish she knew was coming; the wish—not uttered for the first time—to be freed from his bondage.

"Mother," at length said the boy, "I can stand it no longer. I cannot and will not stay at Mr. Ells'. Ever since the day I first went into his house, I've been a slave, and if I have to work there much longer, I know I shall run away, and go to sea, or somewhere else. I'd as leave be in my grave as there." And the child burst into a passionate fit of weeping.

His mother was silent, for she was in deep grief herself. After some minutes had flown, however, she gathered sufficient self-possession to speak to her son in a soothing tone, endeavoring to win him from his sorrows, and cheer up his heart. She told him that time was swift; that in the course of years he would be his own master; that all people had their troubles; with other ready arguments, which though they had little effect in calming her own distress, she hoped would act as a solace on the disturbed temper of the boy. And as the half hour to which he was limited had now elapsed, she took him by the hand and led him to the gate to set forth on his return. The child seemed pacified, though occasionally one of those convulsive sighs that remain after a fit of weeping, would break from his throat. At the gate, he threw his arms about his mother's neck; each pressed a long kiss on the lips of the other, and the youngster bent his steps towards his master's house.

As her child passed out of sight, the widow returned, shut the gate, and entered her lonesome room. There was no light in the old cottage that night; the heart of its occupant was dark and cheerless. Sore agony, and grief, and tears, and convulsive wrestlings were there. The thought of a beloved son condemned to labor—labor that would bend down a man—struggling from day to day under the hard rule of a soulless gold-worshipper; the knowledge that years must pass thus; the sickening idea of her own poverty, and of living mainly on the grudged charity of neighbors—these racked the widow's heart, and made her bed a sleepless one. O, you, who, living in plenty and peace, fret at some little misfortune or some trifling disappointment—behold this spectacle, and blush at your unmanliness! Little do you know of the dark trials (compared to yours as night's great veil to a daylight cloud) that are still going on around you; the pangs of hunger—the faintness of the soul at seeing those we love trampled down, without our having the power to aid them—the wasting away of the body in sickness incurable—and those dull achings of the heart when the consciousness comes upon the poor man's mind, that while he lives he will in all probability live in want and wretchedness.

The boy bent his steps to his employer's as has been said. In his way down the village street, he had to pass a public house, the only one the place contained; and when he came off against it, he heard the sound of a fiddle, drowned however at intervals by much laughter and talking. The windows were up; and, the house standing close to the road, Charles thought it no harm to take a look and see what was going on within. Half-a-dozen footsteps brought him to the low casement, on which he leaned his elbow, and where he had a full view of the room and its occupants. In one corner was an old man known in the village as Black Dave: he it was whose musical performances had a moment before drawn Charles's attention to the tavern; and he it was who now exerted himself in a most violent manner to give, with divers flourishes and extra twangs, a tune popular among that thick-lipped race whose fondness for melody is so well known. In the middle of the room were five or six sailors, some of them quite drunk, and others in the earlier stages of that process; while on benches around were more sailors, and here and there a person dressed in landsmen's attire, but hardly behind the sea-gentlemen in uproariousness and mirth. The individuals in the middle of the room were dancing—that is, they were going through certain contortions and shufflings, varied occasionally by exceeding hearty stamps upon the sanded floor. In short, the whole party were engaged in a drunken frolic, which was in no respect different from a thousand other drunken frolics, except perhaps that there was less than the ordinary amount of anger and quarrelling. Indeed, everyone seemed in remarkably good humor. But what excited the boy's attention more than any other object, was an individual seated on one of the benches opposite, who though evidently enjoying the spree as much as if he were an old hand at such business, seemed in every other particular to be far out of his element. His appearance was youthful; he might have been twenty-one or two. His countenance was intelligent—and had the air of city life and society. He was dressed not gaudily, but in all respects fashionably, his coat being of the finest black broadcloth, his linen delicate and spotless as snow, and his whole aspect a counterpart to those which may be nightly seen in the dress circles of our most respectable theatres. He laughed and talked with the rest; and it must be confessed his jokes, like the most of those that passed current there, were by no means distinguished for their refinement or purity. Near the door, was a small table covered with decanters, and with glasses, some of which had been used but were used again indiscriminately, and a box of very thick and long cigars.

"Come, boys," said one of the sailors, taking advantage of a momentary pause in the hubbub to rap his enormous knuckles on the table, and call attention to himself; the gentleman in question had but one eye, and two most extensive whiskers. "Come, boys, let's take a drink, I know you're all a getting dry, so curse me if you shant have a suck at my expense."

This polite invitation was responded to by a general moving of the company toward the little table, holding the before-mentioned decanters and glasses. Clustering there around, each gentleman helped himself to a very respectable portion of that particular liquor which suited his fancy; and steadiness and accuracy being at that time by no means distinguishing traits of the arms and legs of the party, a goodly amount of the fluid was spilled upon the floor. This piece of extravagance excited the ire of the personage who was treating; and his anger was still further increased when he discovered two or three loiterers who seemed disposed to slight his civil request to drink.

"Walk up boys, walk up. Don't let there be any skulkers among us, or blast my eyes if he shant go down on his marrow bones and gobble up the rum we've spilt. Hallo!" he exclaimed, as he spied Charles, "Hallo! you chap in the window, come here and take a sup."

As he spoke, he stepped to the open casement, put his brawny hands under the boy's armpits, and lifted him into the room bodily.

"There, my lads," he said to his companions, "there's a new recruit for you. Not so coarse a one either," he added as he took a fair view of the boy, who, though not what is called pretty, was fresh, and manly looking, and large for his age.

"Come youngster, take a glass," he continued; and he poured one nearly full of strong brandy.

Now Charles was not exactly frightened, for he was a lively fellow and had often been at the country merry-makings, and with the young men of the place who were very fond of him; but he was certainly rather abashed at his abrupt introduction to the midst of strangers. So, putting the glass aside, he looked up with a pleasant smile in his new acquaintance's face.

"I've no need of anything now," he said, "but I'm just as much obliged to you as if I was."

"Poh! man, drink it down," rejoined the sailor; "drink it down, it won't hurt you." And by way of showing its excellence, the one-eyed worthy drained it himself to the very last drop. Then filling it again he renewed his hospitable efforts to make the lad go through the same operation.

"I've no occasion; beside, it makes my head ache, and I have promised my mother not to drink any," was the boy's answer.

A little irritated by his continued refusals, the sailor, with a loud oath, declared that Charles should swallow the brandy whether he would or no. Placing one of his tremendous paws on the back of the boy's head, with the other he thrust the edge of the glass to his lips, swearing at the same time, that if he shook it so as to spill its contents, the consequences would be of a nature by no means agreeable to his back and shoulders. Disliking the liquor, and angry at the attempt to overbear him, the undaunted child lifted his hand and struck the arm of the sailor with a blow so sudden, that the glass fell and was smashed to pieces on the floor, while the liquid was about equally divided between the face of Charles, the clothes of the sailor, and the sand. By this time the whole of the company had their attention drawn to the scene. Some of them laughed when they saw Charles' undisguised antipathy to the drink; but they laughed still more heartily when he discomfitted the sailor. All of them, however, were content to let the matter go as chance would have it—all but the young man of the black coat, who had before been spoken of. Why was it that from the first moment of seeing him, the young man's heart had moved with a strange feeling of kindness toward the boy? He felt anxious to know more of him—he felt that he should love him. O, it is passing wondrous, how in the hurried walks of life and business, we meet with young beings, strangers, who seem to touch the fountains of our love, and draw forth their swelling waters. The wish to love and to be beloved, which the forms of custom, and the engrossing anxiety for gain, so generally smother, will sometimes burst forth in spite of all obstacles; and, kindled by one, who, till the hour was unknown to us, will burn with a lovely and a pure brightness. No scrap is this of sentimental fiction; ask your own heart, reader, and your own memory, for endorsement to its truth.

Charles stood, his cheek flushed and his heart throbbing, wiping the trickling drops from his face with a handkerchief. At first, the sailor, between his drunkenness and his surprise, was pretty much in the condition of one who is suddenly awakened out of a deep sleep, and cannot call his consciousness about him. When he saw the state of things however, and heard the jeering laugh of his companions, his dull eye, lighting up with anger, fell upon the boy who had withstood him. He seized the child with a grip of iron; he bent Charles half way over, and with the side of his heavy foot, gave him a sharp and solid kick. He was about repeating the performance, for the child hung like a rag in his grasp; but all of a sudden his ears rung as if pistols had snapped close to them; lights of various hues flickered in his eye, (he had but one, it must be remembered,) and a strong propelling power, caused him to move from his position, and keep moving until he was brought up by the wall. A blow—a cuff, given in such a scientific and effectual manner, that the hand from which it came was evidently no stranger to the pugilistic art—had been suddenly planted on the ear of the sailor. It was planted by the young stranger of the black coat. He had watched with interest the proceedings of the sailor and the boy: two or three times he was on the point of interfering, but when he witnessed the kick, his rage was uncontrollable. He sprung from his seat like a mad tiger. Assuming, unconsciously, however, the attitude of a boxer, he struck the sailor in a manner to cause those unpleasant sensations just described; and he would probably have followed up his attack in a method by no means consistent with the sailor's personal ease, had not Charles, now thoroughly terrified, clung round his leg, and prevented his advancing. The scene was a strange one, and for a moment quite a silent one. The company had started from their seats and held startled but quiet positions; in the middle of the room stood the young man, in his not at all ungraceful posture, every nerve strained, and his eyes flashing very brilliantly. He seemed to be rooted like a rock, and clasping him with an appearance of confidence in his protection, hung the boy.

"Dare! you scoundrel!" cried the young man, his voice thick with agitation; "dare to touch this boy again, and I'll batter you till no sense is left in your body."

The sailor, now partially recovered, made some gestures from which it might be inferred that he resented this ungenteel treatment.

"Come on, drunken brute!" continued the angry youth; "I wish you would—you've not had half what you deserve."

Upon sobriety and sense more fully taking their seats in the brains of the one-eyed mariner, however, that worthy determined in his own mind, that it would be most prudent to let the matter drop. Expressing, therefore, his conviction to that effect, adding certain remarks to the purport that he "meant no harm to the lad," that he was surprised at such a gentleman getting so "up about a little piece of fun," and so forth. He proposed that the company should go on with their jollity just as if nothing had happened. In truth, he of the single eye was not a bad hearted fellow; the fiery enemy, whose advances he had so often courted that night, had stolen away his good feelings, and set busy devils at work within him, that might have made his hands do some dreadful deed, had not the stranger interfered.

In a few minutes the frolic of the party was upon its former footing. The young man sat down on one of the benches, with the boy by his side; and, while the rest were loudly laughing and talking, they two held communion together. The stranger learned from Charles all the particulars of his simple story—how his father had died years since—how his mother had worked hard for a bare living, and how he himself for many dreary months had been the bond-child of a hard-hearted, avaricious master. More and more interested, drawing the child close to his side, the young man listened to his plainly told history; and thus an hour passed away. It was now past midnight. The young man told

Charles that on the morrow he would take steps to have him liberated from his servitude; for the present night, he said, it would perhaps be best for the boy to stay and share his bed at the inn; and little persuading did the child need to do so. As they retired to sleep, very pleasant thoughts filled the mind of the young man; thoughts of a worthy action performed; of unsullied affection; thoughts, too—newly awakened ones—of walking in a steadier and wiser path than formerly. All his imaginings seemed to be interwoven with the youth who lay by his side; he folded his arms around him, and, while he slept, the boy's cheek rested on his bosom. Fair were those two creatures in their unconscious beauty—glorious, but yet how differently glorious! One of them was innocent and sinless of all wrong: the other—O to that other, what evil had not been present, either in action or to his desires!

Who was the stranger? To those who, from ties of relationship or otherwise, felt an interest in him, the answer to such a question was not a pleasant theme to dwell upon. His name was Lankton—parentless—a dissipated young man—a brawler—one whose too frequent companions were rowdies, blacklegs, and swindlers. The New-York police officers were not altogether strangers to his countenance; and certain reporters who note the transactions there, had more than once received gratuities for leaving out his name from the disgraceful notoriety of their columns. He had been bred to the profession of medicine: beside that, he had a very respectable income, and his house was in a pleasant street on the west side of the city. Little of his time, however, did Mr. John Lankton spend at his domestic hearth; and the elderly lady who officiated as housekeeper was by no means surprised to have him gone for a week or a month at a time, and she knowing nothing of his whereabout. Living as he did, the young man was an unhappy being. It was not so much that his associates were below his own capacity, for Lankton, though sensible and well-bred, was by no means talented or refined—but that he lived without any steady purpose—that he had no one to attract him to his home—that he too easily allowed himself to be tempted—which caused his life to be of late one continued scene of dissatisfaction. This dissatisfaction he sought to drive away (ah! foolish youth!) by mixing in all kinds of parties and places where the object was pleasure. On the present occasion, he had left the city a few days before, and was passing the time at a place near the village where Charles and his mother lived. He had that day fallen in with those who were his companions in the tavern spree—and thus it happened that they were all together: for Lankton hesitated not to make himself at home with any associates that suited his fancy.

The next morning, the poor widow rose from her sleepless cot, and from that lucky trait in our nature which makes one extreme follow another, she set about her daily toil with a lightened heart. Ellis, the farmer, rose too, short as the nights were, an hour before day; for his God was gain, and a prime article of his creed was to get as much work as possible from everyone around him. He roused up all his people, and finding that Charles had not been home the preceding night, he muttered threats against him, and calling a messenger, to whom he hinted that any minutes which he stayed beyond a most exceeding short period, would be subtracted from his breakfast time, dispatched him to the widow's to find what was her son about.

What was he about? With one of the brightest and earliest rays of the warm sun a gentle angel entered his apartment, and hovering over the sleepers on invisible wings, looked down with a pleasant smile and blessed them. Then noiselessly taking a stand by the bed, the angel bent over the boy's face, and whispered strange words into his ear: thus it came that he had beautiful visions. No sound was heard but the slight breathing of those who slumbered there in each others arms; and the angel paused a moment, and smiled another and a doubly sweet smile as he drank in the scene with his large soft eyes. Bending over again to the boy's lips, he touched them with a kiss, as the languid wind touches a flower. He seemed to be going now—and yet he lingered. Twice or thrice he bent over the brow of the young man—and went not. Now the angel was troubled; for he would have pressed the young man's forehead with a kiss, as he did the child's; but a spirit from the Pure Country, who touches anything tainted by evil thoughts, does it at the risk of having his breast pierced with pain, as with a barbed arrow. At that moment a very pale bright ray of sunlight darted through the window and settled on the young man's features. Then the beautiful spirit knew that permission was granted him: so he softly touched the young man's face with his, and silently and swiftly wafted himself away on the unseen air.

In the course of the day Ellis was called upon by young Lankton, and never perhaps in his life was the farmer more puzzled than at the young man's proposals—his desire to provide for a boy who could do him no pecuniary good—and his willingness to disburse money for that purpose. In that department of Ellis's structure where the mind was, or ought to have been situated, there never had entered the slightest thought assimilating to those which actuated the young man in his proceedings in this business. Yet Ellis was a church member and a county officer.

The widow too, was called upon, not only that day, but the next and the next.

It needs not to particularize the subsequent events of Lankton's and the boy's history: how the reformation of the profligate might be dated to begin from that time; how he gradually severed the guilty ties that had so long galled him—how he enjoyed his own home, and loved to be there, and why he loved to be there; how the close knit love of the boy and him grew not slack with time; and how, when at length he became head of a family of his own, he would shudder when he thought of his early danger and escape.

Loved reader, own you the moral of this simple story? Draw it forth—pause a moment, ere your eye wanders to a more bright and eloquent page—and dwell upon it.

BERVANCE: OR, FATHER AND SON.

ALMOST incredible as it may seem, there is more truth than fiction in the following story. Whatever of the latter element may have been added, is for the purpose of throwing that disguise around the real facts of the former, which is due to the feelings of a respectable family. The principal parties alluded to have left the stage of life many years since; but I am well aware there are not a few yet alive, who, should they, as is very probable, read this narration, will have their memories carried back to scenes and persons of a much more substantial existence than the mere creation of an author's fancy. I have given it the form of a confession in the first person, partly for the sake of convenience, partly of simplicity, but chiefly because such was the form in which the main incidents were a long time ago repeated to me by my own informant. It is a strange story—the true solution of which will probably be found in the supposition of a certain degree of unsoundness of mind, on the one part, manifesting itself in the morbid and unnatural paternal antipathy; and of its reproduction on the other, by the well known though mysterious law of hereditary transmission.

W. W.

My appointed number of years has now almost sped. Before I sink to that repose in the bosom of our great common mother, which I have so long and earnestly coveted, I will disclose the story of a life which one fearful event has made, through all its latter stages, a continued stretch of wretchedness and remorse. There may possibly be some parents to whom it may serve as a not useless lesson.

I was born, and have always lived, in one of the largest of our Atlantic cities. The circumstances of my family were easy; I received a good education, was intended by my father for mercantile business, and upon attaining the proper age, obtained from him a small but sufficient capital; and in the course of a few years from thus starting, found myself sailing smoothly on the tide of fortune. I married; and, possessed of independence and domestic comfort, my life was a happy one indeed. Time passed on; we had several children; when about twenty years after our marriage my wife died. It was a grievous blow to me, for I loved her well; and the more so of late, because that a little while before, at short intervals, I had lost both my parents.

Finding myself now at that period of life when ease and retirement are peculiarly soothing, I purchased an elegant house in a fashionable part of the city; where, surrounding myself and my family with every resource that abundance and luxury can afford for happiness, I settled myself for life—a life which seemed to promise every prospect of a long enjoyment. I had my sons and daughters around me; and objecting to the boarding-school system, I had their education conducted under my own roof, by a private tutor who resided with us. He was a mild, gentlemanly man, with nothing remarkable about his personal appearance, unless his eyes might be called so. They were gray—large, deep, and having a softly beautiful expression, that I have never seen in any others; and which, while they at times produced an extraordinary influence upon me, and yet dwell so vividly in my memory, no words that I can use could exactly describe. The name of the tutor was Alban.

Of my children, only two were old enough to be considered anything more than boys and girls. The eldest was my favorite. In countenance he was like the mother, whose first-born he was; and when she died, the mantle of my affections seemed transferred to him, with a sadly undue and unjust degree of preference over the rest. My second son, Luke, was bold, eccentric, and high-tempered. Strange as it may seem, notwithstanding a decided personal resemblance to myself, he never had his father's love. Indeed, it was only by a strong effort that I restrained and concealed a positive aversion. Occasions seemed continually to arise wherein the youth felt disposed to thwart me, and make himself disagreeable to me. Every time I saw him, I was conscious of something evil in his conduct or disposition. I have since thought that a great deal of all this existed only in my own imagination, warped and darkened as it was, and disposed to look upon him with an "evil eye." Be that as it may, I was several times made very angry by what I felt sure were intended to be wilful violations of my rule, and contemptuous taunts toward me for that partiality to his brother which I could not deny. In the course of time, I grew to regard the heedless boy with a feeling almost amounting—I shudder to make the confession—to hatred. Perhaps, for he was very cunning, he saw it, and, conscious that he was wronged, took the only method of revenge that was in his power.

I have said that he was eccentric. The term is hardly strong enough to mark what actually was the case with him. He occasionally had spells which approached very nearly to complete derangement. My family physician spoke learnedly of regimen, and drugs, and courses of treatment which, if carefully persevered in, might remove the peculiarity. He said, too, that cases of that kind were dangerous, frequently terminating in confirmed insanity. But I laughed at him, and told him his fears were idle. Had it been my favorite son instead of Luke, I do not think I would have passed by the matter so contentedly.

Matters stood as I have described them for several years. Alban, the tutor, continued with us; as fast as one grew up, so as to be beyond the need of his instructions, another appeared in the vacant place. The whole family loved him dearly, and I have no doubt he repaid their affection; for he was a gentle-hearted creature, and easily won. Luke and he seemed always great friends. I blush now, as I acknowledge that this was the only thing by which Alban excited my displeasure.

I shall pass over many circumstances that occurred in my family, having no special relation to the event which, in the present narrative, I have chiefly in view. One of my favorite amusements was afforded by the theatre. I kept a box of my own, and frequently attended, often giving my family permission also to be present. Luke I seldom allowed to go. The excuse that I assigned to myself and to others was, that he was of excitable temperament, and the acting would be injurious to his brain. I fear the privilege was withheld quite as much from vindictiveness toward him, and dislike of his presence on my own part. So Luke himself evidently thought and felt. On a certain evening—(were it last night, my recollection of it all could not be more distinct)—a favorite performer was to appear in a new piece; and it so happened that every one of us had arranged to attend—everyone but Luke. He besought me earnestly that he might go with the rest—reminded me how rarely such favors were granted him—and even persuaded Alban to speak to me on the subject.

"Your son," said the tutor, "seems so anxious to partake of this pleasure, and has set his mind so fully upon it, that I really fear, sir, your refusal would excite him more than the sight of the play."

"I have adopted a rule," said I, "and once swerving from it makes it no rule at all."

"Mr. Bervance will excuse me," he still continued, "if I yet persevere in asking that you will allow Luke this indulgence, at least for this one evening. I am anxious and disturbed about the boy,—and should even consider it as a great personal favor to myself."

"No, sir," I answered, abruptly, "it is useless to continue this conversation. The young man cannot go, either from considerations of his pleasure or yours."

Alban made no reply; he colored, bowed slightly, and I felt his eye fixed upon me with an expression I did not at all like, though I could not analyze it. I was conscious, however, that I had said too much; and if the tutor had not at that moment left the room, I am sure I should have apologized for my rudeness.

We all went to the theatre. The curtain had hardly risen, when my attention was attracted by someone in the tier above, and right off against my box, coming noisily in, talking loudly, and stumbling along, apparently on purpose to draw the eyes of the spectators. As he threw himself into a front seat, and the glare of the lamps fell upon his face, I could hardly believe my eyes when I saw it was Luke. A second and a third observation were necessary to convince me. There he sat, indeed. He looked over to where I was seated, and while my sight was riveted upon him in unbounded astonishment, he deliberately rose—raised his hand to his head—lifted his hat, and bowed low and long—a cool sarcastic smile playing on his features all the time,—and finally breaking into an actual laugh, which even reached my ears. Nay—will it be believed!—the foolish youth had even the effrontery to bring down one of the wretched outcasts who are met with there, and seat himself full in our view—he laughing and talking with his companion so much to the annoyance of the house, that a police officer was actually obliged to interfere! I felt as if I should burst with mortification and anger.

At the conclusion of the tragedy we went home. Reader, I cannot dwell minutely on what followed. At a late hour my rebellious boy returned. Seemingly bent upon irritating me to the utmost, he came with perfect nonchalance into the room where I was seated. The remainder of that night is like a hateful dream in my memory, distinct and terrible, though shadowy. I recollect the sharp, cutting, but perfectly calm rejoinders he made to all my passionate invectives against his conduct. They worked me up to phrensy, and he smiled all the more calmly the while. Half maddened by my rage, I seized him by the collar, and shook him. My pen almost refuses to add—but justice to myself demands it—the Son felled the Father to the earth with a blow! Some blood even flowed from a slight wound caused by striking my head, as I fell against a projecting corner of furniture—and the hair that it matted together was gray!

What busy devil was it that stepped noiselessly round the bed, to which I immediately retired, and kept whispering in my ears all that endless night? Sleep forsook me. Thoughts of a deep revenge—a fearful redress—but it seemed to me hardly more fearful than the crime—worked within my brain. Then I turned, and tried to rest, but vainly. Some spirit from the abodes of ruin held up the provocation and the punishment continually before my mind's eye. The wretched youth had his strange fits: those fits were so thinly divided from insanity, that who should undertake to define the difference? And for insanity was there not a prison provided, with means and appliances, confinement, and, if need be, chains and scourges? For a few months it would be nothing more than wholesome that an unnatural child, a brutal assaulter of his parent, should taste the discipline of such a place. Before my eyes closed, my mind had resolved on the scheme—a scheme so cruel, that as I think of it now, my senses are lost in wonder that any one less than fiend could have resolved to undertake it.

The destinies of evil favored me. The very next morning Luke had one of his strange turns, brought on, undoubtedly, by the whirl and agitation of the previous day and night. With the smooth look and the quiet tread with which I doubt not Judas looked and trod, I went into his room and enjoined the attendants to be very careful of him. I found him more violently affected than at any former period. He did not know me; I felt glad that it was so, for my soul shrank at its own intentions, and I could not have met his conscious eye. At the close of the day, I sent for a physician; not him who generally attended my family, but one of those obsequious gentlemen who bend and are pliant like the divining-rod, that is said to be attracted by money. I sent, too, for some of the officers of the lunatic asylum. Two long hours we were in conversation. I was sorry, I told them, very sorry; it was a dreadful grief to me; the gentlemen surely could not but sympathize in my distress; but I felt myself called upon to yield my private feelings. I felt it best for my unhappy son to be, for a time at least, removed to the customary place for those laboring under his miserable disease. I will not say what other measures I took— what tears I shed. Oh, to what a depth may that man be sunk who once gives bad passions their swing! The next day, Luke was taken from my dwelling to the asylum, and confined in what was more like a dungeon, than a room for one used to all the luxurious comforts of life.

Days rolled on. I do not think anyone suspected aught of what really was the case. Evident as it had been that Luke was not a favorite of mine, no person ever thought it possible that a father could place his son in a mad-house, from motives of any other description than a desire to have him cured. The children were very much hurt at their brother's unfortunate situation. Alban said nothing; but I knew that he sorrowed in secret. He frequently sought, sometimes with success, to obtain entrance to Luke; and after a while began to bring me favorable reports of the young man's recovery. One day, about three weeks after the event at the theatre, the tutor came to me with great satisfaction on his countenance. He had just returned from Luke, who was now as sane as ever. Alban said he could hardly get away from the young man, who conjured him to remain, for solitude there was a world of terror and agony. Luke had besought him, with tears streaming down his cheeks, to ask me to let him be taken from that place. A few days longer residence there, he said, a conscious witness of its horrors, and he should indeed be its fit inmate forever.

The next morning I sent private instructions to the asylum, to admit no person in Luke's apartment without an order from me. Alban was naturally very much surprised, as day after day elapsed, and I took no measures to have my son brought home. Perhaps, at last, he began to suspect the truth; for in one of the interviews we had on the subject, those mild and beautiful eyes of his caused mine to sink before them, and he expressed a determination, dictated as he said by an imperious duty, in case I did not see fit to liberate the youth, to take some decided steps himself. I talked as smoothly and as sorrowfully as possible—but it was useless.

"My young friend, I am sure," said he, "has received all the benefits he can possibly derive from the institution, and I do not hesitate to say, any longer continuance there may be followed by dangerous—even fatal consequences. I cannot but think," and the steadfast look of that gray eye settled at me, as if it would pierce my inmost soul, "that Mr. Bervance desires to see his unlucky child away from so fearful an abode; and I have no doubt that I shall have his approval in any proper and necessary measures for that purpose."

I cursed him in my heart, but I felt that I had to submit. So I told him that if in two days more Luke did not have any relapse, I would then consider it safe to allow him to be brought home.

The swift time flew and brought the evening of the next day. I was alone in the house, all the family having gone to a concert, which I declined attending, for music was not then suited to my mood. The young people stayed later than I had expected; I walked the floor till I was tired, and then sat down on a chair. It was a parlor at the back of the house, with long, low windows opening into the garden. There and then, in the silence of the place, I thought for the first time of the full extent of the guilt I had lately been committing. It pressed upon me, and I could not hide from my eyes its dreadful enormity. But it became too painful, and I rose, all melted with agonized yet tender emotions, and determined to love my injured boy from that hour as Father should love Son. In the act of rising, my eyes were involuntarily cast toward a large mirror, on the chimney-piece. Was it a reflection of my own conscience, or a horrid reality? My blood curdled as I saw there an image of the form of my son—my cruelly treated Luke—but oh, how ghastly, how deathly a picture! I turned, and there was the original of the semblance. Just inside one of the windows stood the form, the pallid, unwashed, tangly-haired, rag-covered form of Luke Bervance. And that look of his—there was no deception there—it was the vacant, glaring, wild look of a maniac.

"Ho, ho!"

As I listened, I could hardly support myself, for uncontrollable horror.

"My son, do you not know me? I am your father," I gasped.

"You are Flint Serpent. Do you know me, Flint? A little owl screeched in my ear, as I came through the garden, and said you would be glad to see me, and then laughed a hooting laugh. Speak low," he continued in a whisper; "big eyes and bony hands are out there, and they would take me back again. But you will strike at them, Flint, and scatter them, will you not? Sting them with poison; and when they try to seize me, knock them down with your heart, will you not?"

"Oh, Christ! what a sight is this!" burst from me, as I sank back into the chair from which I had risen, faint with agony. The lunatic started as I spoke, and probably something like recollection lighted up his brain for a moment. He cast a fierce look at me:

"Do you like it?" he said, with a grim smile; "it is of your own doing. You placed me in a mad-house. I was not mad; but when I woke, and breathed that air, and heard the sounds, and saw what is to be seen there—Oh, now I am mad! Curse you! it is your work. Curse you! Curse you!"

I clapped my hands to my ears, to keep out the appalling sounds that seemed to freeze my very blood. When I took them away, I heard the noise of the street door opening, and my children's voices sounding loud and happily. Their maniac brother heard them also. He sprang to the window.

"Hark!" he said; "they are after me, Flint. Keep them back. Rather than go there again, I would jump into a raging furnace of fire!" He glided swiftly into the garden, and I heard his voice in the distance. I did not move, for every nerve seemed paralyzed.

"Keep them back, Flint! It is all your work! Curse you!"

When my family came into the apartment, they found me in a deep swoon, which I fully recovered from only at the end of many minutes.

My incoherent story, the night, and the strangeness of the whole affair, prevented any pursuit that evening, though Alban would have started on one, if he had had any assistance or clue. The next morning, the officers of the asylum came in search of the runaway. He had contrived a most cunning plan of escape, and his departure was not found out till daylight.

My story is nearly ended. We never saw or heard of the hapless Luke more. Search was extensively made, and kept up for a long time; but no tidings were elicited of his fate. Alban was the most persevering of those who continued the task, even when it became hopeless. He inserted advertisements in the newspapers, sent emissaries all over the country, had handbills widely distributed, offering a large reward; but all to no purpose. The doom, whatever it was, of the wretched young man, is shrouded in a mantle of uncertainty as black as the veil of the outer darkness in which his form had disappeared on that last memorable night; and in all likelihood it will now never be known to mortal.

A great many years have gone by since these events. To the eyes of men, my life and feelings have seemed in no respect different from those of thousands of others. I have mixed with company—laughed and talked—eaten and drunk; and, now that the allotted term is closing, must prepare to lay myself in the grave. I say I have lived many years since then, and have laughed and talked. Let no one suppose, however, that time has banished the phantoms of my busy thoughts, and allowed me to be happy. Down in the inward chamber of my soul there has been a mirror—large, and very bright. It has pictured, for the last thirty years, a shape, wild and haggard, and with tangly hair—the shape of my maniac son. Often, in the midst of society, in the public street, at my own table, and in the silent watches of the night, that picture stands out in glaring brightness; and, without a tongue, tells me that it is all my work, and repeats that terrible cursing which, the last time the tyrant and victim stood face to face together, rang from the lips of the Son, and fell like a knell of death on the ear of the Father.

———

THE TOMB-BLOSSOMS.

A PLEASANT, fair-sized country village,—a village embosomed in trees, with old churches, one tavern, kept by a respectable widow, long, single-storied farm-houses, their roofs mossy, and their chimneys smoke black,—a village with much grass, and shrubbery, and no mortar, nor bricks, nor pavements, nor gas—no newness: that is the place for him who wishes life in its flavor and its bloom. Until of late, my residence has been in such a place.

Man of cities! what is there in all your boasted pleasure—your fashions, parties, balls, and theatres, compared to the simplest of the delights we country folk enjoy? Our pure air, making the blood swell and leap with buoyant health; our labor and our exercise; our freedom from the sickly vices that taint the town; our not being racked with notes due, or the fluctuations of prices, or the breaking of banks; our manners of sociality, expanding the heart, and reacting with a wholesome effect upon the body;—can anything which citizens possess balance these?

One Saturday, after paying a few days visit at New York, I returned to my quarters in the country inn. The day was hot, and my journey a disagreeable one. I had been forced to stir myself beyond comfort, and despatch my affairs quickly, for fear of being left by the cars. As it was, I arrived panting and covered with sweat, just as they were about to start. Then for many miles I had to bear the annoyance of the steam-engine smoke; and it seemed to me that the vehicles kept swaying to and fro on the track, with a more than usual motion, on purpose to distress my jaded limbs. Out of humor with myself and everything around me, when I came to my travel's end, I refused to partake of the comfortable supper which my landlady had prepared for me; and rejoining to the good woman's look of wonder at such an unwonted event, and her kind inquiries about my health, with a sullen silence, I took my lamp, and went my way to my room. Tired and head-throbbing, in less than half a score of minutes after I threw myself on my bed, I was steeped in the soundest slumber.

When I awoke, every vein and nerve felt fresh and free. Soreness and irritation had been swept away, as it were, with the curtains of the night; and the accustomed tone had returned again. I arose and threw open my window. Delicious! It was a calm, bright Sabbath morning in May. The dew-drops glittered on the grass; the fragrance of the apple-blossoms which covered the trees floated up to me; and the notes of a hundred birds discoursed music to my ear. By the rays just shooting up in the eastern verge, I knew that the sun would be risen in a moment. I hastily dressed myself, performed my ablutions, and sallied forth to take a morning walk.

Sweet, yet sleepy scene! No one seemed stirring. The placid influence of the day was even now spread around, quieting everything, and hallowing everything. I sauntered slowly onward, with my hands folded behind me. I passed round the edge of a hill, on the rising elevation and top of which was the burial-ground. On my left, through an opening in the trees, I could see at some distance the ripples of our beautiful bay; on my right, was the large and ancient field for the dead. I stopped and leaned my back against the fence, with my face turned toward the white marble stones a few rods before me. All I saw was far from new to me; and yet I pondered upon it. The entrance to that place of tombs was a kind of arch—a rough-hewn but no doubt hardy piece of architecture, that had stood winter and summer over the gate there, for many, many years. O, fearful arch! if there were for thee a voice to utter what has passed beneath and near thee; if the secrets of the earthy dwelling that to thee are known could be by thee disclosed—whose ear might listen to the appalling story and its possessor not go mad with terror?

Thus thought I; and strangely enough, such imagining marred not in the least the sunny brightness which spread alike over my mind and over the landscape. Involuntarily as I mused, my look was cast to the top of the hill. I saw a figure moving. Could someone beside myself be out so early, and among the tombs?—What creature odd enough in fancy to find pleasure there, and at such a time? Continuing my gaze, I saw that the figure was a woman. She seemed to move with a slow and a feeble step, passing and repassing constantly between two and the same graves, which were within half a rod of each other. She would bend down and appear to busy herself a few moments with the one; then she would rise, and go to the second, and bend there, and employ herself as at the first. Then to the former one, and then to the second again. Occasionally the figure would pause a moment, and stand back a little, and look steadfastly down upon the graves, as if to see whether her work were done well. Thrice I saw her walk with a tottering gait, and stand midway between the two, and look alternately at each. Then she would go to one and arrange something, and come back to the midway place, and gaze first on the right and then on the left, as before. The figure evidently had some trouble in suiting things to her mind. Where I stood, I could hear no noise of her footfalls; nor could I see accurately enough to tell what she was doing. Had a superstitious man beheld the spectacle, he would possibly have thought that some spirit of the dead, allowed the night before to burst its cerements, and wander forth in the darkness, had been belated in returning, and was now perplexed to find its coffin-house again.

Curious to know what was the woman's employment, I undid the simple fastenings of the gate, and walked over the rank wet grass toward her. As I came near, I recognised her for an old, a very old inmate of the poor-house, named Delaree. Stopping a moment, while I was yet several yards from her, and before she saw me, I tried to call to recollection certain particulars of her history which I had heard a great while past. She was a native of one of the West India islands, and, before I who gazed at her was born, had with her husband come hither to settle and gain a livelihood. They were poor; most miserably poor. Country people, I have noticed, seldom like foreigners. So this man and his wife, in all probability, met much to discourage them. They kept up their spirits, however, until at last their fortunes became desperate. Famine and want laid iron fingers upon them. They had no acquaintance; and to beg they were ashamed. Both were taken ill; then the charity that had been so slack came to their destitute abode, but came too late. Delaree died, the victim of poverty. The woman recovered, after a while; but for many months was quite an invalid, and was sent to the alms-house, where she had ever since remained.

This was the story of the aged creature before me; aged with the weight of seventy winters. I walked up to her. By her feet stood a large rude basket, in which I beheld leaves and buds. The two graves which I had seen her passing between so often were covered with flowers—the earliest but sweetest flowers of the season. They were fresh, and wet, and very fragrant—those delicate soul-offerings. And this, then, was her employment. Strange! Flowers, frail and passing, grasped by the hand of age, and scattered upon a tomb! White hairs, and pale blossoms, and stone tablets of Death!

"Good morning, mistress," said I, quietly.

The withered female turned her eyes to mine, and acknowledged my greeting in the same spirit wherewith it was given.

"May I ask whose graves they are that you remember so kindly?"

She looked up again; probably catching, from my manner, that I spoke in no spirit of rude inquisitiveness; and answered,

"My husband's."

A manifestation of a fanciful taste, thought I, this tomb-ornamenting, which she probably brought with her from abroad. Of course, but one of the graves could be her husband's; and one, likely, was that of a child, who had died and been laid away by its father.

"Whose else?" I asked.

"My husband's," replied the aged widow.

Poor creature! her faculties were becoming dim. No doubt her sorrows and her length of life had worn both mind and body nearly to the parting.

"Yes, I know," continued I, mildly; "but there are two graves. One is your husband's, and the other is———"

I paused for her to fill the blank.

She looked at me for a minute, as if in wonder at my perverseness; and then answered as before,

"My husband's. None but my Gilbert's."

"And is Gilbert buried in both?" said I.

She appeared as if going to answer, but stopped again, and did not. Though my curiosity was now somewhat excited, I forebore to question her further, feeling that it might be to her a painful subject. I was wrong, however. She had been rather agitated at my intrusion, and her powers flickered for a moment. They were soon steady again; and, perhaps gratified with my interest in her affairs, she gave me in a few brief sentences the solution of the mystery. When her husband's death occurred, she was herself confined to a sick bed, which she did not leave for a long while after he was buried. Still longer days passed before she had permission, or even strength, to go into the open air. When she did, her first efforts were essayed to reach Gilbert's grave. What a pang sunk to her heart when she found it could not be pointed out to her! With the careless indifference which is shown to the corpses of outcasts, poor Delaree had been thrown into a hastily dug hole, without any one noting it, or remembering which it was. Subsequently, several other paupers were buried in the same spot; and the sexton could only show two graves to the disconsolate woman, and tell her that her husband's was positively one of the twain. During the latter stages of her recovery, she had looked forward to the consolation of coming to his tomb as to a shrine, and wiping her tears there; and it was bitter that such could not be. The miserable widow even attempted to obtain the consent of the proper functionaries that the graves might be opened, and her anxieties put at rest! When told that this could not be done, she determined in her soul that at least the remnant of her hopes and intentions should not be given up. Every Sunday morning, in the mild seasons, she went forth early, and gathered fresh flowers, and dressed both the graves. So she knew that the right one was cared for, even if another shared that care. And lest she should possibly bestow the most of this testimony of love on him whom she knew not, but whose spirit might be looking down invisible in the air, and smiling upon her, she was ever careful to have each tomb adorned in an exactly similar manner. In a strange land, and among a strange race, she said, it was like communion with her own people to visit that burial-mound.

"If I could only know which to bend over when my heart feels heavy," thus finished the sorrowing being as she rose to depart, "then it would be a happiness. But perhaps I am blind to my dearest mercies. God in his great wisdom may have sent that I should not know which grave was his, lest grief over it should become too common a luxury for me, and melt me away."

I offered to accompany her, and support her feeble steps; but she preferred that it should not be so. With languid feet she moved on. I watched her pass through the gate and under the arch; I saw her turn, and in a little while she was hidden from my view. Then I carefully parted the flowers upon one of the graves, and sat down there, and leaned my face in my open hands and thought.

What a wondrous thing is woman's love! Oh Thou whose most mighty attribute is the Incarnation of Love, I bless Thee that Thou didst make this fair disposition in the human heart, and didst root it there so deeply that it is stronger than all else, and can never be torn out! Here is this aged wayfarer, a woman of trials and griefs, decrepit, sore, and steeped in poverty; the most forlorn of her kind; and yet, through all the storm of misfortune, and the dark cloud of years settling upon her, the Memory of her Love hovers like a beautiful spirit amid the gloom; and never deserts her, but abides with her while life abides. Yes; this creature loved: this wrinkled, skinny, gray-haired crone had her heart to swell with passion, and her pulses to throb, and her eyes to sparkle. Now, nothing remains but a Lovely Remembrance, coming as of old, and stepping in its accustomed path, not to perform its former object, or former duty—but from long habit. Nothing but that!—Ah! is not that a great deal?

And the buried man—he was happy to have passed away as he did. The woman—she was the one to be pitied. Without doubt she wished many times that she were laid beside him. And not only she, thought I, as I cast my eyes on the solemn memorials around me; but at the same time there were thousands else on earth, who panted for the Long Repose, as a tired child for the night. The grave—the grave—what foolish man calls it a dreadful place? It is a kind friend, whose arms shall compass us round about, and while we lay our heads upon his bosom, no care, temptation, nor corroding passion shall have power to disturb us. Then the weary spirit shall no more be weary; the aching head and aching heart will be strangers to pain; and the soul that has fretted and sorrowed away its little life on earth will sorrow not any more. When the mind has been roaming abroad in the crowd, and returns sick and tired of hollow hearts, and of human deceit—let us think of the grave and of death, and they will seem like soft and pleasant music. Such thoughts then soothe and calm our pulses; they open a peaceful prospect before us. I do not dread the grave. There is many a time when I could lay down, and pass my immortal part through the valley of the shadow, as composedly as I quaff water after a tiresome walk. For what is there of terror in taking our rest? What is there here below to draw us with such fondness? Life is the running of a race—a most weary race, sometimes. Shall we fear the goal, merely because it is shrouded in a cloud?

I rose, and carefully replaced the parted flowers, and bent my steps homeward.

If there be any sufficiently interested in the fate of the aged woman, that they wish to know further about her, for those I will add, that ere long her affection was transferred to a Region where it might receive the reward of its constancy and purity. Her last desire—and it was complied with—was that she should be placed midway between the two graves.

———

THE LAST OF THE SACRED ARMY.

THE memory of the WARRIORS of our FREEDOM!—let us guard it with a holy care. Let the mighty pulse which throbs responsive in a nation's heart at utterance of that nation's names of glory, never lie languid when their deeds are told or their example cited. To him of the Calm Gray Eye, selected by the Leader of the Ranks of Heaven as the instrument for a people's redemption;—to him, the bright and brave, who fell in the attack at Breed's;—to him, the nimble-footed soldier of the swamps of Santee;—to the young stranger from the luxuries of his native France;—to all who fought in that long weary fight for disenthralment from arbitrary rule—may our star fade, and our good angel smile upon us no more, if we fail to chamber them in our hearts, or forget the method of their dear-won honor!

For the fame of these is not as the fame of common heroes. The mere gaining of battles—the chasing away of an opposing force—wielding the great energies of bodies of military—rising proudly amid the smoke and din of the fight—and marching the haughty march of a conqueror,—all this, spirit-stirring as it may be to the world, would fail to command the applause of the just and discriminating. But such is not the base whereon American warriors found their title to renown. Our storied names are those of the Soldiers of Liberty; hardy souls, incased in hardy bodies— untainted with the effeminacy of voluptuous cities, patient, enduring much for principle's sake, and wending on through blood, disease, destitution, and prospects of gloom, to attain the Great Treasure.

Years have passed; the sword-clash and the thundering of the guns have died away; and all personal knowledge of those events—of the fierce incentives to hate, and the wounds, and scorn, and the curses from the injured, and the wailings from the prisons—lives now but in the memory of a few score gray-haired men; whose number is, season after season, made thinner and thinner by death. Haply, long, long will be the period ere our beloved country shall witness the presence of such or similar scenes again. Haply, too, the time is arriving when War, with all its train of sanguinary horrors, will be a discarded custom among the nations of earth. A newer and better philosophy—teaching how evil it is to hew down and slay ranks of fellow-men, because of some disagreement between their respective rulers—is melting old prejudices upon this subject, as warmth in spring melts the frigid ground.

The lover of his race—did he not, looking abroad in the world, see millions whose swelling hearts are all crushed into the dust beneath the iron heel of oppression; did he not behold how kingcraft and priestcraft stalk abroad over fair portions of the globe, and forge the chain, and rivet the yoke; and did he not feel that it were better to live in one flaming atmosphere of carnage than slavishly thus—would offer up nightly prayers that this new philosophy might prevail to the utmost, and the reign of peace never more be disturbed among mankind.

On one of the anniversaries of our national independence, I was staying at the house of an old farmer, about a mile from a thriving country town, whose inhabitants were keeping up the spirit of the occasion with great fervor. The old man himself was a thumping patriot. Early in the morning, my slumbers had been broken by the sharp crack of his ancient musket, (I looked upon that musket with reverence, for it had seen service in the war,) firing salutes in honor of the day. I am free to confess, my military propensities were far from strong enough (appropriate as they might have been considered at such a time) to suppress certain peevish exclamations toward the disturber of my sweet repose. In the course of the forenoon, I attended the ceremonials observed in the village; sat, during the usual patriotic address, on the same bench with a time-worn veteran that had fought in the contest now commemorated; witnessed the evolutions of the uniform company; and returned home with a most excellent appetite for my dinner.

The afternoon was warm and drowsy. I ensconced myself in my easy-chair, near an open window; feeling in that most blissful state of semi-somnolency, which it is now and then, though rarely, given to mortals to enjoy. I was alone, the family of my host having gone on some visit to a neighbor. The bees hummed in the garden, and among the flowers that clustered over the window frame; a sleepy influence seemed to imbue everything around; occasionally the faint sound of some random gun-fire from the village would float along, or the just perceptible music of the band, or the tra-a-a-ra of a locust. But these were far from being jars to the quiet spirit I have mentioned.

Insensibly, my consciousness became less and less distinct; my head leaned back; my eyes closed; and my senses relaxed from their waking vigilance. I slept.

* * * *How strange a chaos is sometimes the outset to a dream!—There was the pulpit of the rude church, the scene of the oration—and in it a grotesque form whom I had noticed as the drummer in the band, beating away as though calling scattered forces to the rescue. Then the speaker of the day pitched coppers with some unshorn hostler boys; and the grave personage who had opened the services with prayer, was half stripped and running a foot-race with a tavern loafer. The places and the persons familiar to my morning excursion about the country town, appeared as in life; but in situations all fantastic and out of the way.*

After a while, what I beheld began to reduce itself to more method. With the singular characteristic of dreams, I knew—I could not tell how—that thirty years elapsed from the then time, and I was among a new generation. Beings by me never seen before, and some with shrivelled forms, bearing an odd resemblance to men whom I had known in the bloom of manhood, met my eyes.

Methought I stood in a splendid city. It seemed a gala day. Crowds of people were swiftly wending along the streets and walks, as if to behold some great spectacle or famous leader.

"Whither do the people go?" said I to a Shape who passed me, hurrying on with the rest.

"Know you not," answered he, "that the Last of the Sacred Army may be seen to-day?"

And he hastened forward, apparently fearful lest he might be late.

Among the dense ranks, I noticed many women, some of them with infants in their arms. Then there were boys, beautiful creatures, struggling on, with a more intense desire even than the men. And as I looked up, I saw at some distance, coming toward the place where I stood, a troop of young females, the foremost one bearing a wreath of fresh flowers. The crowd pulled and pushed so violently, that this party of girls were sundered from one another, and she who carried the wreath being jostled, her flowers were trampled to the ground.

"O, hapless me!" cried the child; and she began to weep.

At that moment, her companions came up; and they looked frowningly when they saw the wreath torn.

"Do not grieve, gentle one," said I to the weeping child. "And you," turning to the others, "blame her not. There bloom more flowers, as fair and fragrant as those which lie rent beneath your feet."

"No," said one of the little troop, "it is now too late."

"What mean you?" I asked.

The children looked at me in wonder.

"For whom did you intend the wreath?" continued I.

"Heard you not," rejoined one of them, "that to-day may be seen the Last of His Witnesses? We were on our way to present this lovely wreath—and she who should give it, was to say, that fresh and sweet, like it, would ever be His memory in the souls of us, and of our countrymen."

And the children walked on.

Yielding myself passively to the sway of the current, which yet continued to flow in one huge human stream, I was carried through street after street, and along many a stately passage, the sides of which were lined by palace-like houses. After a time, we came to a large open square, which seemed to be the destination—for there the people stopped. At the further end of this square stood a magnificent building, evidently intended for public purposes; and in front of it a wide marble elevation, half platform and half porch. Upon this elevation were a great many persons, all of them in standing postures, except one, an aged, very aged man, seated in a throne-like chair. His figure and face showed him to be of a length of years seldom vouchsafed to his kind; and his head was thinly covered with hair of a silvery whiteness.

Now, near me stood one whom I knew to be a learned philosopher; and to him I addressed myself for an explanation of these wonderful things.

"Tell me," said I, "who is the ancient being seated on yonder platform."

The person to whom I spoke stared in my face surprisedly.

"Are you of this land," said he, "and have not heard of him—the Last of the Sacred Army?"

"I am ignorant," answered I, "of whom you speak, or of what Army."

The philosopher stared a second time; but soon, when I assured him I was not jesting, he began telling me of former times, and how it came to be that this white-haired remnant of a past age was the object of so much honor. Nor was the story new to me—as may it never be to any son of America.

We edged our way close to the platform. Immediately around the seat of the ancient soldier stood many noble-looking gentlemen, evidently of dignified character and exalted station. As I came near, I heard them mention a name—that name which is dearest to our memories as patriots.

"And you saw the Chief with your own eyes?" said one of the gentlemen.

"I did," answered the old warrior.

And the crowd were hushed, and bent reverently, as if in a holy presence.

"I would," said another gentleman, "I would you had some relic which might be as a chain leading from our hearts to his."

"I have such a relic," replied the aged creature; and with trembling fingers he took from his bosom a rude medal, suspended round his neck by a string. "This the Chief gave me," continued he, "to mark his good-will for some slight service I did The Cause."

"And has it been in his hands?" asked the crowd, eagerly.

"Himself hung it around my neck," said the veteran.

Then the mighty mass was hushed again, and there was no noise—but a straining of fixed eyes, and a throbbing of hearts, and cheeks pale with excitement—such excitement as might be caused in a man's soul by some sacred memorial of one he honored and loved deeply.

Upon the medal were the letters "G. W."

"Speak to us of him, and of his time," said the crowd.

A few words the old man uttered; but few and rambling as they were, the people listened as to the accents of an oracle.

Then it was time for him to stay there no longer. So he rose, assisted by such of the bystanders whose rank and reputation gave them a right to the honor, and slowly descended. The mass divided, to form a passage for him and his escort, and they passed forward. And as he passed, the young boys struggled to him, that they might take his hand, or touch his garments. The women, too, brought their infants, to be placed for a moment in his arms; and every head was uncovered.

I noticed that there was little shouting, or clapping of hands—but a deep-felt sentiment of veneration seemed to pervade them, far more honorable to its object than the loudest acclamations.

In a short time, as the white-haired ancient was out of sight, the square was cleared, and I stood in it with no companion but the philosopher.

"Is it well," said I, "that such reverence be bestowed by a great people on a creature like themselves? The self-respect each one has for his own nature might run the risk of effacement, were such things often seen. Besides, it is not allowed that man pay worship to his fellow."

"Fear not," answered the philosopher; "the occurrences you have just witnessed spring from the fairest and manliest traits in the soul. Nothing more becomes a nation than paying its choicest honors to the memory of those who have fought for it, or labored for its good. By thus often bringing up their examples before the eyes of the living, others are incited to follow in the same glorious path. Do not suppose, young man, that it is by sermons and oft-repeated precepts we form a disposition great or good. The model of one pure, upright character, living as a beacon in history, does more benefit than the lumbering tomes of a thousand theorists.

"No: it is well that the benefactors of a state be so kept alive in memory and in song, when their bodies are mouldering. Then will it be impossible for a people to become enslaved; for though the strong arm of their old defender come not as formerly to the battle, his spirit is there, through the power of remembrance, and wields a better sway even than if it were of fleshly substance."

*** *The words of the philosopher sounded indistinctly to my ears—and his features faded, as in a mist. I awoke; and looking through the window, saw that the sun had just sunk in the west—two hours having passed away since the commencement of my afternoon slumber.*

———

THE CHILD-GHOST; A STORY OF THE LAST LOYALIST.

WERE it not from the evidence of my own ears and observation, I could hardly believe that any considerable number of persons exist among us, who give credence to accounts of spectres and disembodied spirits appearing from the dead;—yet there are many such people, especially in our country places. Though the schools are gradually thrusting aside these superstitious relics of a by gone time, it will perhaps be long before their influence is effectually rooted out. Guilt or ignorance, working through imagination, has magic power; and the ideal forms through which terror is thus stricken, produces a panic in the minds of their victims, as real as if those forms were of perceptible substance.

The story I am going to tell is a traditional reminiscence of a country place, in my rambles about which I have often passed the house, now unoccupied and mostly in ruins, that was the scene of the transaction. I cannot, of course, convey to others that particular kind of influence, which is derived from my being so familiar with the locality and with the very people whose grandfathers or fathers were contemporaries of the actors in the drama I shall transcribe. I must hardly expect, therefore, that to those who hear it through the medium of my pen, the narration will possess as life-like and interesting a character as it does to myself.

On a large and fertile neck of land that juts out in the Sound which stretches to the south-east of New York city, there stood, in the latter part of the last century, an old-fashioned country residence. It had been built by one of the first settlers of this section of the New World; and its occupant was originally owner of the extensive tract lying adjacent to his house, and pushing into the very bosom of the salt waters.

It was during the troubled times which marked our American Revolution that the incidents occurred which are the foundation of my story. Some time before the commencement of the war, the owner, whom I shall call Vanhome, was taken sick and died. For years before his death he had lived a widower; and his child, an only one, a lad of ten years old, was thus left an orphan. By his father's will, this child was placed implicitly under the guardianship of an uncle, a middle-aged man, who had been of late a resident in the family.

As if to verify the truth of the ancient proverb, which declares that evils, when once started on their path, follow each other thick and fast—not two years elapsed after the parents were laid away to their last repose, before another grave had to be prepared for the son—the fair and lovely child who had been so haplessly deprived of their fostering care.

The period had now arrived when the great national convulsion burst forth. Sounds of strife, and the clash of arms, and the angry voices of disputants, were borne along by the air; and week after week grew to louder and still louder clamor. Families were divided; adherents to the crown, and ardent upholders of the rebellion, were often found in the bosom of the same domestic circle. Vanhome, the uncle spoken of as guardian to the young heir, was a man who leaned to the stern, the high-handed, and the severe. He soon became known among the most energetic of the loyalists. So violent were his sentiments, that, leaving the estate which he had so fortunately inherited from his brother and nephew, he joined the forces of the British king. Thenceforward, whenever his old neighbors heard of him, it was as being engaged in the cruellest outrages, the boldest inroads, or the most determined attacks upon the army of his countrymen, or their peaceful settlements.

Though pleasant for an American mind to dwell upon the traits,—the unshaken patriotism, the lofty courage, and the broad love of liberty exhibited by our fathers in their memorable struggle, I shall pass over the relation.

Eight years brought the rebel States and their leaders to that glorious epoch when the last remnant of a monarch's rule was to leave their shores—when the last waving of the royal standard was to flutter as it should be hauled down from the staff, and its place filled by the proud testimonial of our warriors' success.

Pleasantly over the autumn fields shone the November sun, when a horseman, of somewhat military look, plodded slowly along the road that led to the old Vanhome farm-house. There was nothing peculiar in his attire, unless it might be a red scarf which he wore tied round his waist. He was a dark-featured, sullen-eyed man; and as his glance was thrown restlessly to the right and left, his whole manner appeared to be that of a person moving amid familiar and accustomed scenes. Occasionally he stopped, and looking long and steadily at some object that attracted his attention, muttered to himself, like one in whose breast busy thoughts were moving. His course was evidently to the homestead itself, at which in due time he arrived. He dismounted, led his horse to the stables, and then, without knocking, though there were evident signs of occupancy around the building, the traveller made his entrance as composedly and boldly as though he were master of the whole establishment.

Now it had happened that the house being in a measure deserted for many years, and the successful termination of the strife rendering it probable that the Vanhome estate would be confiscated to the new government,—an aged, poverty-stricken couple had been encouraged by the neighbors to take possession as tenants of the place. Their name was

Gills; and these people the traveller found upon his entrance were likely to be his host and hostess. Holding their right as they did by so slight a tenure, they ventured to offer no opposition when the stranger signified his intention of passing several hours there.

The day wore on, and the sun went down in the west. Still the interloper made no signs of departing. But as the night fell, (whether the darkness was congenial to his sombre thoughts, or whether it merely chanced so,) he seemed to grow more affable and communicative.

"Tell me," said he to his aged host, when they were all sitting around the ample hearth, at the conclusion of their evening meal, "tell me something to while away the hours."

"Ah! sir," answered Gills, "this is no place for new or interesting events to happen. We live here from year to year, and, at the end of one, we find ourselves at about the same place which we filled in the beginning."

"Can you relate nothing, then," rejoined the guest—and a singular smile passed over his features; "can you say nothing about your own place? this house or its former inhabitants, or former history?"

The old man glanced across to his wife, and a look expressive of sympathetic feeling started in the face of each.

"It is an unfortunate story, sir," said Gills, "and may cast a chill upon you, instead of the pleasant feeling which it would be best to foster when in strange walls."

"Strange walls!" echoed he of the red scarf; and for the first time since his arrival, he half laughed, but it was not the laugh which comes from a man's heart.

"You must know, sir," continued Gills, "I am myself a sort of intruder here. The Vanhomes—that was the name of the former residents and owners—I have never seen; for when I came to these parts the last Mr. Vanhome had left, to join the red-coat soldiery. I am told that he is to sail with them for foreign lands, now that the war is ended, and his property almost certain to pass into other hands."

As the old man went on, the stranger cast down his eyes, and listened with an appearance of great interest, though a transient smile, or a brightening of the eye, would occasionally disturb the serenity of his deportment.

"The old occupants of this place," continued the white-haired narrator, "were well off in the world, and bore a good name among their neighbors. The brother of Sergeant Vanhome, now the only one of the name, died ten or twelve years since, leaving a son—a child so small, that the father's will made provision for his being brought up by his uncle, whom I mentioned but now as of the British army. He was a strange man, this uncle; disliked by all who knew him, passionate, vindictive, and, it was said, very avaricious, even from his childhood.

"Well; not long after the death of the parents, dark stories began to be circulated about cruelty, and punishment, and whippings, and starvation, inflicted by the new master upon his nephew. People who had business at the homestead would frequently, when they came away, relate the most fearful things of its manager, and how he misused his brother's child. It was half hinted that he strove to get the youngster out of the way, in order that the whole estate might fall into his own hands. As I told you before, however, nobody liked the man; and perhaps they judged him too uncharitably.

"After things had gone on in this way for some time, a countryman, a laborer, who was hired to do farm-work upon the place, one evening observed that the little orphan Vanhome was more faint and pale even than usual, for he was always delicate, and that is one reason why I think it possible that his death, of which I am now going to tell you, was but the result of his own weak constitution, and nothing else.

"The laborer slept that night at the farm-house. Just before the time at which they usually retired to bed, this person, feeling tired and sleepy with his day's toil, took his light, and wended his way to rest. In going to his place of repose, he had to pass a chamber—the very chamber where you, sir, are to sleep to-night—and there he heard the voice of the orphan child, uttering half-suppressed exclamations, as if in pitiful entreaty. Upon stopping, he heard also the tones of the elder Vanhome, but they were harsh and bitter. The whacking sound of blows followed. As each one fell, it was accompanied by a groan or a shriek; and so they continued for some time. Shocked and indignant, the countryman would have burst open the door and interfered to prevent this brutal proceeding; but he bethought him that he might get himself into trouble, and perhaps find that he could do no good after all, and so he passed on to his room.

"Well, sir; the following day the child did not come out among the work-people as usual. He was taken very ill. No physician was sent for until the next afternoon; and though one arrived in the course of the succeeding night, it was too late—the poor boy died before morning.

"People talked threateningly upon the subject, but nothing could be proved against Vanhome. At one period there were efforts made to have the whole affair investigated. Perhaps such a proceeding would have taken place, had not every one's attention been swallowed up by the rumors of difficulty and war, which at that time were beginning to disturb the country.

"Vanhome joined the army of the king. His enemies said that he feared to be on the side of the rebels, because if they were routed his property would be taken from him. But events have shown, that if this was indeed what he dreaded, it has happened to him from the very means which he took to prevent it."

The old man paused. He had quite wearied himself with so long talking. For some minutes there was unbroken silence.

"Did you say that Vanhome had left this land and sailed for Europe?" at length asked the stranger; who, when Gills concluded, had raised his face, pale, and with eyes glittering like one in great perturbation.

"So we hear," returned the old man.

Again there was silence, which no one seemed inclined to break.

Presently, the stranger signified his intention of retiring for the night. He rose, and his host took a light for the purpose of ushering him to his apartment.

"What of this chamber which you mentioned?" said the traveller, pausing as he stood with his back to the fire, and looking not into the face of the old man, but as it were into vacancy.

The host started, and it was evident the question had awakened agitating thoughts in his mind; for his face blanched a little, and his glance turned feverishly from object to object.

"It is said," answered he, in a low stealthy tone, "that the spirit of the little orphan child haunts that chamber in the silent hours of night!"

The stranger wheeled, and looked full into the face of the speaker. A convulsive spasm passed over his features, and from his eyes came the flashing of condensed rage and hideous terror.

"Hell!" uttered he, furiously, "am I to be taunted by ghosts, and placed amid the spectres of puling brats? Find me, hoary thief!—find me some other sleeping place; else will I have you dragged forth and lashed—lashed before the whole regiment!"

His cheeks were white with excitement; ferocity gleamed in every look and limb; and the frightened Gills and his wife shrank back in very fear that he would do them some bodily harm. They thought him mad; his words were so incoherent and strange.

But not quicker passed away is the lightning's flash—not in the swiftest night-storm does a cloud flit more quickly over the face of the moon—than was the clearing up of the stranger's countenance, and the clothing of his face again in its former mantle of indifference.

"Forgive me!" said he, with a bland smile, "I am too hasty. In truth, I have a horror of these superstitious stories; they fret me. But no matter. Do not think I am so silly as to fear this child-spirit you have spoken of. Such nonsense is for the ignorant and the credulous. Again I ask pardon for my rudeness. Let me now be shown to this chamber—this haunted chamber. I am weary. Good night, mistress!"

And without waiting for an answer, he of the red scarf hastily pushed the old man through the door, and they passed to the sleeping room.

When Gills returned to his accustomed situation in the large arm-chair by the chimney hearth, his ancient help-mate had retired to rest. With the simplicity of their times, the bed stood in a kind of alcove, just out of the same room where the three had been seated during the last few hours; and now the remaining two talked together about the singular events of the evening. As the time wore on, Gills showed no disposition to leave his cozy chair; but sat toasting his feet, and bending over the coals—an enjoyment that was to his mind very pleasant and satisfactory.

Gradually the insidious heat and the lateness of the hour began to exercise their influence over the old man. That drowsy indolent feeling which everyone has experienced in getting thoroughly heated through by close contact with a glowing fire, spread in each vein and sinew, and relaxed its tone. He leaned back in his chair and slept.

For a long time his repose went on quietly and soundly. He could not tell how many hours elapsed; but a while after midnight, the torpid senses of the slumberer were awakened by a startling shock. It was a cry as of a strong man in his agony—a shrill, not very loud cry, but fearful, and creeping into the blood, like cold, sharp, polished steel. The old man raised himself in his seat and listened—at once fully awake. For a minute, all was the solemn stillness of midnight. Then rose that horrid tone again—wailing and wild, and making the hearer's hair stand on end. As it floated along to the chamber—borne through the darkness and stillness—it brought to the mind of Gills thoughts of the howlings of damned spirits, and the death-rattle of murdered men, and the agonies of the drowning, and the hoarse croak of the successful assassin.

He sat almost paralyzed in his chair. Then came an interval; and then another of those terrible shrieks. One moment more, and the trampling of hasty feet sounded in the passage outside. The door was thrown open, and the form of the stranger, more like a corpse than living man, rushed into the room.

"He is there!" said the quivering wretch, pointing with his finger, and speaking in low hoarse tones; "he is there, in his little shroud! And he smiled and looked gently upon me with those blue eyes of his—O, how much sharper than a thousand frowns!"

The man shook, like one in a great ague, and his jaws clashed against each other.

"All white!" continued the miserable, conscience-stricken creature; "all white, and with the grave-clothes around him!—One shoulder was bare, and I saw," he whispered, "I saw blue streaks upon it. It was horrible, and I cried aloud. He stepped toward me! He came to my very bed-side; his small hand was raised, and almost touched my face. I could not bear it, and fled."

The miserable man bent his head down upon his bosom; convulsive rattlings shook his throat; and his whole frame wavered to and fro, like a tree in a storm. Bewildered and shocked, Gills looked at his apparently deranged guest, and knew not what answer to make, or what course of conduct to pursue.

"Do you not believe it?" furiously exclaimed the stranger, with a revulsion of feeling, in consistence with his character; "do you think me a child, to be frightened by a bugbear?—Come!" continued he, seizing the alarmed old man by the shoulder; "come hither, and let your own eyes be blasted with the sight!"

And dragging the unresisting Gills, he strode to the door, and dashed it open with a loud and echoing clang.

The house was one of that old-fashioned sort, still to be met with occasionally in country villages, the ground floor of which was comprised of two rooms, divided by a hall—the door of each room being off against the other; so that the old man and his companion had a full view of the adjoining apartment. Though there was no light there, Gills fancied he could see everything distinctly.

In one corner stood the bed from which the stranger had started—its coverlets and sheets all tumbled and half dragged down on the floor. A few feet on one side of its head, was the hearth-stone; and the sight thereon, as Gills strained his eyes to behold it, was drunk in with chilling terror to his heart.

Upon that hearth-stone stood the form of a boy, some ten years old. His face was wan and ghastly, but very beautiful; his hair light and wavy; and he was apparelled in the habiliments of the tomb. As the appalled Gills looked, he felt that the eyes of the pale child were fixed upon him and his companion—fixed, not as in anger, but with a gentle sorrow. From one shoulder the fearful dress had fallen aside, and the appearance of gashes and livid streaks was visible.

"See you?" harshly shrieked the stranger, as if maddened by the sight; "I have not dreamed—he is there, in his snowy robes—he comes to mock me. And look you!" he crouched and recoiled, "does he not step this way again? I shall go mad! If he but touches me with that little hand, I am mad! Away, spectre! boy-phantom, away! or I die too upon this very floor!"

And thrusting out his arms and his extended fingers, and bending down his eyes, as men do when shading them from a glare of lightning—he staggered from the door, and in a moment further, dashed madly through the passage which led through the kitchen into the outer road. The old man heard the noise of his flying footsteps, sounding fainter and fainter in the distance, and then, retreating, dropped his own exhausted limbs into the chair from which he had been aroused so terribly. It was many minutes before his energies recovered their accustomed tone again. Strangely enough, his wife, unawakened by the stranger's ravings, still slumbered on as profoundly as ever.

Pass we on to a far different and almost as thrilling a scene—the embarkation of the British troops for the distant land whose monarch was never more to wield the sceptre over a kingdom lost by his imprudence and tyranny. With frowning brow and sullen pace, the martial ranks moved on. Boat after boat was filled; and as each discharged its complement in the ships that lay heaving their anchors in the stream, it returned, and was soon filled with another load. And at length it became time for the last soldier to lift his eye, and take a last glance at the broad banner of England's pride, which flapped its folds from the top of the highest staff on the Battery. Proud spectacle! May the flag which was planted in the place of the blood-red cross, waft out to the wind for ages and ages yet—and the nations of earth number not one so glorious as that which claims the star-gemmed symbol of liberty for its token!

As the warning sound of a trumpet called together all who were laggards—those taking leave of friends, and those who were arranging their own private affairs, left until the last moment—a single horseman was seen furiously dashing down the street. A red scarf tightly encircled his waist. He made directly for the shore, and the crowd there gathered started back in wonderment as they beheld his dishevelled appearance and his ghastly face. Throwing himself violently from his saddle, he flung the bridle over the animal's neck, and gave him a cut with a small riding-whip. He made for the boat; one minute later, and he had been left. They were pushing the keel from the landing—the stranger sprang—a space of two or three feet already intervened—he struck on the gunwale—and the Last Soldier of King George had left the American shores.

———

Reuben's Last Wish.

IF the reader supposes that I am going to tell a story full of plot, interest, and excitement, let him peruse no farther than these two or three lines—for he will be disappointed. A simple tale—a narration not half so strange as people frequently see exemplified in their ordinary walks—is all I have to offer. Yet, as the greatest and profoundest truths are often most plain to the senses of men—in the same resemblance, my "Reuben" may haply teach a moral and plant a seed of wholesome instruction.

Not many weeks since, I happened to be in a country village, sixty miles, more or less, to the north of our great new world metropolis, New York. Towards sundown, I heard from the keeper of the inn where I was staying, that there was to be a temperance lecture in the place that night. The scene of the meeting was the school house; and having no other means of employing my time, I determined to attend.

At the appointed hour, I did so. The lecture itself was rather a prosy affair, but fortunately short; when it concluded, several persons, apparently residents thereabout, rose and made remarks, partly advice, and partly transcripts of facts which had come under their observation. One of the speakers, a man considerably advanced in life, I listened to with much interest. After the exercises were over, I took occasion to introduce myself, and converse for some time with this man; and upon what I heard him say in the public meeting—the particulars he furnished me at our private interview—and, also, the additional facts I gathered from the people of the place, the subsequent day—I have based the narrative which follows.

Franklin Slade, a handsome, healthy American farmer, possessed, at the age of thirty years, a comfortable estate, a fair reputation, a tolerably well filled purse—and could boast that he owed no debts which he was not able to pay on the instant. He had a prudent, good tempered wife, and two children, sons, one eight years old and the other three.

Through one of the thousand painted snares, which ministers of sin ever stand ready to tempt frailty withal, Slade, about this period, fell into a habit of tippling. At first, he would indulge himself but rarely, and that to a limited degree; but the fatal taste grew upon him, and in the course of years, the man was a drunkard, habitual and confirmed.

Franklin Slade, a bloated, red faced fellow, at the age of forty years, had his estate mortgaged for half its value—no man cared for his good will—his purse held not a dollar—and creditors insulted him daily. The once ruddy cheek of his wife was withered and pale from much sorrow; and her eye had lost its accustomed brightness. His eldest son, Slade had struck in a fit of drunken passion; the boy was high tempered—he left his father's house—shipped as a sailor to some far distant port—and thenceforward they never heard of him again. Little Reuben, the other son, was an invalid, and, (the bitter truth may as well be told,) an invalid through his father's wretched sensuality. Some time previous, the child being with Slade several miles away, the farmer drank so deeply, that he soon felt in no condition to get home. Reuben was kept out the whole night— a cold, rainy one. He was naturally delicate, and the exposure produced an effect on him from which he never recovered.

There is something very solemn in the sickness of children. The ashiness, and the moisture on the brow, and the film over the eye balls— what man can look upon the sight, and not feel his heart awed within him? Children, I have noticed too, increase in beauty as their illness deepens. The angels, it may be, are already vesting them with the garments they shall wear in the Pleasant Land.

Slade, to do him justice, was deeply grieved that the fruits of his folly fell thus upon the innocent Reuben, whom he loved much. Yet his infatuation had rooted so deeply, that he desisted in no respect from his dissolute practices. He scoffed at the efforts of the temperance advocates, who were becoming numerous and successful in the town—as they occasionally strove to bring him to their faith, and besought him to sign the pledge. His son very often joined his voice for the same purpose; entreaties and arguments, however, were alike futile.

Visiting, whenever his strength permitted, the meetings of the Temperance people, and reading and talking frequently upon the subject, Reuben before long entered with much enthusiasm into the new movement. He was an intelligent lad—and that he had seen what an evil thing drunkenness was, may well be imagined from the facts already given.

"I would," said the child one day to his mother, "I would have this paper bordered prettily with silk, and a fine ribbon bow at the top."

He held in his hand a Temperance pledge, with a picture at the top, and a blank space at the bottom for the names of signers.

"You are whimsical, my dear," said the matron, as she took the paper; "why do you desire so needless a thing done?"

"I hardly know myself," answered he, "yet please do it, mother. Ask me not why—let it be a whim."

And he smiled faintly.

And the sickening thought came over the woman's soul, that ere long she would probably not have the pleasant trouble of listening to the poor fellow's vagaries. She stepped hastily from the room, weeping.

In a day or two the Temperance pledge was edged tastily with a border of blue silk, and at each end, a piece of ribbon of the same color. The child was pleased: he took it and put it aside.

Days, months rolled on. The dwelling of Slade was a substantial old farm-house, a pleasant place, in the rear of which stretched a large garden. As it was now the season of advanced spring, the trees began to bud out and bloom there—the flowers put forth their beautiful tints—and the grass donned its darkest green. Birds sang there too—the robin, and the black bird, and the fanciful bob-o-link.

In the middle of the garden was a fine, grassy patch, shaded by a stupendous tree: leaning against the trunk of the tree had been built a long, wide, rustic seat. It was very fair, that spot—dreamy, warm, and free from annoyance of any kind.

Reuben, frequently walking here among the flowers and shrubs, would admire this grass plot, and stop, and resting himself on the seat, would remain a long hour enjoying the delight of the scene—not such delight as children are generally fond of, romping, and playing, and laughing—but a noiseless, motionless delight, in keeping with the place.

Still the days rolled on—and Reuben grew no better, but worse. Physicians seemed of little benefit. The only method of producing a favorable effect upon his spirits—and that was merely temporary—seemed to be to let him have quite his own way in all his fancies and his actions. Still he was never querulous or fretful.

One notion of the sick boy—though an odd one, they acquiesced in it—was to have a kind of couch made for him; and when he was too weak for walking about, to have it carried in the garden, on the favorite grass plot, that he might rest on it there.

For a time they kept somebody by him while he lay thus, lest his illness might take a fatal turn.—As, however, nothing of that kind occurred, and he lingered day after day without alteration, they relaxed somewhat from having a watcher by his garden bed. Now and then they would leave him, though not long—for a mother's affection is to her child like a needle to its magnet—though it may vibrate aside a little on occasions, it ever settles back again, truly and constantly.

Reuben, indeed, preferred being alone. He would get them to bring him large bunches of flowers, roses, and the fragrant carnation, and the delicate lily—which he would arrange fancifully about him: then, when he grew tired of such simple pastime, he would sink back, and lie long, long minutes, gazing on the bright sky above, and watching the changes of the clouds as they melted from tint to tint, and changed from form to form.

It grew at length to be, that the very birds, that had their nests thereabout, or sought fruit from the neighboring trees, became accustomed to the presence of Reuben, and hopped down upon his couch, and would rest upon his extended hand. They sometimes sat upon the branches over him, and would sing blithely and long—which was very sweet to the little invalid.

One morning it happened that the child fell asleep while he lay alone upon his bed in the garden. And while he slept, he dreamed a beautiful dream. He thought that he, after passing, he could not tell how, for a great way through the air, landed at last on the borders of a fair country, where he wandered about for some time. The place was more delightful than ever entered the imagination of man, with fadeless verdure, and bright day, and summer eternal. By and by he entered a city, thronged with people, such as it charmed his eyes to behold—all clothed in raiment like fleecy clouds, and each with a glittering star upon his forehead. Here he was accosted by a Being, even more splendid than the others, and told in tones of soft music, that he should not be sick any more as on earth, but be taken to the presence of the Great King. Then he was conducted by the Being, who led the way, holding his hand, through many bright avenues and shining halls—and at last ushered into a mighty space, whose limits the gazer's eye could not scan, filled with millions of the winged ones—and in the midst a throne, whence light flashed like double lightning.

And then the sleeper awoke.

Several persons were standing around him. One, the village doctor, had apparently been holding his wrist—for he let it fall as soon as Reuben opened his eyes. The boy felt strangely faint, yet he smiled as he saw his parents, and briefly told them his vision. His mother was sobbing aloud.

"My son," she cried, in uncontrollable agony; "my son! you die!"

And the father bowed him low, as a tree by the tempest—and thick tears rippled between the fingers which he held before his eyes. O, it is a fearful thing to see a man in desperate grief!

Reuben comprehended the truth; else why that cloud—that dark consciousness shadowing his soul? He lay drowsily; a few drops of sweat started upon his forehead, and he began to grow insensible to perception or feeling of any kind. It was a state something resembling sleep, yet different from it—it was without pain—it was DEATH.

For what moved the child thus uneasily, and sped his eyes from one to another? With some effort he turned himself, raised his arm to his pillow, and drew something from underneath it, he unrolled a paper edged with silk, of the hue of the clouds overhead.

All was the silence of the grave. The dying boy slowly lifted the tremulous forefinger of his right hand, as he held the document in his left—that finger quivered for a moment in the air—the eyes of the child, now becoming glassy with death damp, were fixedly cast toward his father's face; he smiled pleasantly—and as an indistinct gurgle sounded from his throat, the uplifted finger calmly settled downward, and rested, pointing upon the blank space at the bottom of the Temperance pledge.

And so he passed away.

When the solemnity of the scene, and the impressiveness of the closing incident, which for a while awed them motionless and silent, allowed other influences to act, they looked, and saw Reuben lying before them a cold corpse. His finger was pointed still. A gentle look lingered upon his face; the perfume of flowers filled the air; and from the western sky came a ray of light, left by the departing sun, investing the spot, as it were, with a halo of glory.

———

A LEGEND OF LIFE AND LOVE.

A VERY cheerless and fallacious doctrine is that which teaches to deny the yielding to natural feelings, righteously directed, because the consequences may be trouble and grief, as well as satisfaction and pleasure. The man who lives on from year to year, jealous of ever placing himself in a situation where the chances can possibly turn against him—ice, as it were, surrounding his heart, and his mind too scrupulously weighing in a balance the results of giving way to any of those propensities his Creator has planted in his heart—may be a philosopher, but can never be a happy man.

Upon the banks of a pleasant river stood a cottage, the residence of an ancient man whose limbs were feeble with the weight of years and of former sorrow. In his appetites easily gratified, like the simple race of people among whom he lived, every want of existence was supplied by a few fertile acres. Those acres were tilled and tended by two brothers, grandsons of the old man, and dwellers also in the cottage. The parents of the boys lay buried in a grave nearby.

Nathan, the elder, had hardly seen his twentieth summer. He was a beautiful youth. Glossy hair clustered upon his head, and his cheeks were very brown from sunshine and open air. Though the eyes of Nathan were soft and liquid, like a girl's, and his cheeks curled with a voluptuous swell, exercise and labor had developed his limbs into noble and manly proportions. The bands of hunters, as they met sometimes to start off together after game upon the neighboring hills, could hardly show one among their number who in comeliness, strength, or activity, might compete with the youthful Nathan.

Mark was but a year younger than his brother. He, too, had great beauty.

In course of time the ancient sickened, and knew that he was to die. Before the approach of the fatal hour, he called before him the two youths, and addressed them thus:

"The world, my children, is full of deceit. Evil men swarm in every place; and sorrow and disappointment are the fruits of intercourse with them. So wisdom is wary.

"And as the things of life are only shadows, passing like the darkness of a cloud, twine no bands of love about your hearts. For love is the ficklest of the things of life. The object of our affection dies, and we thenceforth languish in agony; or perhaps the love we covet dies, and that is more painful yet.

"It is well never to confide in any man. It is well to keep aloof from the follies and impurities of earth. Let there be no links between you and others. Let not any being control you through your dependence upon him for a portion of your happiness. This, my sons, I have learned by bitter experience, is the teaching of truth."

Within a few days afterward, the old man was placed away in the marble tomb of his kindred, which was built on a hill by the shore.

Now the injunctions given to Nathan and his brother—injunctions frequently impressed upon them before by the same monitorial voice—were pondered over by each youth in his inmost heart. They had always habitually respected their grandsire: whatever came from his mouth, therefore, seemed as the words of an oracle not to be gainsayed.

Soon the path of Nathan chanced to be sundered from that of Mark.

And the trees leaved out, and then in autumn cast their foliage; and in due course leaved out again, and again, and many times again—and the brothers met not yet.

Two score years and ten! what change works over earth in such a space as two score years and ten!

As the sun, an hour ere his setting, cast long slanting shadows to the eastward, two men, withered, and with hair thin and snowy, came wearily up from opposite directions, and stood together at a tomb built on a hill by the borders of a fair river. Why do they start, as each casts his dim eyes toward the face of the other? Why do tears drop down their cheeks, and their frames tremble even more than with the feebleness of age? They are the long separated brethren, and they enfold themselves in one another's arms.

"And yet," said Mark, after a few moments, stepping back, and gazing earnestly upon his companion's form and features, "and yet it wonders me that thou art my brother. There should be a brave and beautiful youth, with black curls upon his head, and not those pale emblems of decay. And my brother should be straight and nimble—not bent and tottering as thou."

The speaker cast a second searching glance—a glance of discontent.

"And I," rejoined Nathan, "I might require from my brother, not such shrivelled limbs as I see,—and instead of that cracked voice, the full swelling music of a morning heart—but that half a century is a fearful melter of comeliness and of strength; for half a century it is, dear brother, since my hand touched thine, or my gaze rested upon thy face."

Mark sighed, and answered not.

Then, in a little while, they made inquiries about what had befallen either during the time past. Seated upon the marble by which they had met, Mark briefly told his story.

"I bethink me, brother, many, many years have indeed passed over since the sorrowful day when our grandsire, dying, left us to seek our fortunes amid a wicked and a seductive world.

"His last words, as thou, doubtless, dost remember, advised us against the snares that should beset our subsequent journeyings. He portrayed the dangers which lie in the path of love; he impressed upon our minds the folly of placing confidence in human honor; and warned us to keep aloof from too close communion with our kind. He then died, but his instructions live, and have ever been present in my memory.

"Dear Nathan, why should I conceal from you that at that time I loved. My simple soul, ungifted with the wisdom of our aged relative, had yielded to the delicious folly, and the brown-eyed Eva was my young heart's choice. O brother, even now,—the feeble and withered thing I am,—dim recollections, pleasant passages, come forth around me, like the joy of old dreams. A boy again, and in the confiding heart of a boy, I walk with Eva by the river's banks. And the gentle creature blushes at my protestations of love, and leans her cheek upon my neck. The regal sun goes down in the west, and we gaze upon the glory of the clouds that attend his setting, and while we look at their fantastic changes, a laugh sounds out, clear like a flute, and merry as the jingling of silver bells. It is the laugh of Eva."

The eye of the old man glistened with unwonted brightness. He paused, sighed, the brightness faded away, and he went on with his narration.

"As I said, the dying lessons of him whom we reverenced were treasured in my soul. I could not but feel their truth. I feared that if I again stood beside the maiden of my love, and looked upon her face, and listened to her words, the wholesome axioms might be blotted from my thought, so I determined to act as became a man: from that hour I never have beheld the brown-eyed Eva.

"I went amid the world. Acting upon the wise principles which our aged friend taught us, I looked upon everything with suspicious eyes. Alas! I found it but too true that iniquity and deceit are the ruling spirits of men.

"Some called me cold, calculating, and unamiable; but it was their own unworthiness that made me appear so to their eyes. I am not—you know, my brother—I am not, naturally, of proud and repulsive manner; but I was determined never to give my friendship merely to be blown off again, it might chance, as a feather by the wind; nor interweave my course of life with those that very likely would draw all the advantage of the connexion, and leave me no better than before.

"I engaged in traffic. Success attended me. Enemies said that my good fortune was the result of chance,—but I knew it the fruit of the judicious system of caution which governed me in matters of business, as well as of social intercourse.

"My brother, thus have I lived my life. Your look asks me if I have been happy. Dear brother, truth impels me to say no. Yet assuredly, if few glittering pleasures ministered to me on my journey, equally few were the disappointments, the hopes blighted, the trusts betrayed, the faintings of the soul, caused by the defection of those in whom I had laid up treasures.

"Ah, my brother, the world is full of misery!"

The disciple of a wretched faith ceased his story, and there was silence a while.

Then Nathan spake:

"In the early years," he said, "I too loved a beautiful woman. Whether my heart was more frail than thine, or affection had gained a mightier power over me, I could not part from her I loved without the satisfaction of a farewell kiss. We met,—I had resolved to stay but a moment,—for I had chalked out my future life after the fashion thou hast described thine.

"How it was I know not, but the moment rolled on to hours; and still we stood with our arms around each other.

"My brother, a maiden's tears washed my stern resolves away. The lure of a voice rolling quietly from between two soft lips, enticed me from remembrance of my grandsire's wisdom. I forgot his teachings, and married the woman I loved.

"Ah! how sweetly sped the seasons! We were blessed. True, there came crossings and evils; but we withstood them all, and holding each other by the hand, forgot that such a thing as sorrow remained in the world.

"Children were born to us—brave boys and fair girls. Oh, Mark, that, that is a pleasure—that swelling of tenderness for our offspring—which the rigorous doctrines of your course of life have withheld from you!

"Like you, I engaged in trade. Various fortune followed my path. I will not deny but that some in whom I thought virtue was strong, proved cunning hypocrites, and worthy no man's trust. Yet are there many I have known, spotless, as far as humanity may be spotless.

"Thus, to me, life has been alternately dark and fair. Have I lived happy?—No, not completely; it is never for mortals so to be. But I can lay my hand upon my heart, and thank the Great Master, that the sunshine has been far oftener than the darkness of the clouds.

"Dear brother, the world has misery—but it is a pleasant world still, and affords much joy to the dwellers!"

As Nathan ceased, his brother looked up in his face, like a man unto whom a simple truth had been for the first time revealed.

———

THE ANGEL OF TEARS.

HIGH, high in space floated the angel Alza. Of the spirits who minister in heaven Alza is not the chief; neither is he employed in deeds of great import, or in the destinies of worlds and generations. Yet if it were possible for envy to enter among the Creatures Beautiful, many would have pined for the station of Alza. There are a million million invisible eyes which keep constant watch over the earth—each Child of Light having his separate duty. Alza is one of the Angels of Tears.

Why waited he, as for commands from above?

There was a man upon whose brow rested the stamp of the guilt of Cain. The man had slain his brother. Now he lay in chains awaiting the terrible day when the doom he himself had inflicted should be meted to his own person.

People of the Black Souls!—beings whom the world shrinks from, and whose abode, through the needed severity of the law, is in the dark cell and massy prison—it may not be but that ye have, at times, thoughts of the beauty of virtue, and the blessing of a spotless mind. For if we look abroad in the world, and examine what is to be seen there, we will know, that in every human heart resides a mysterious prompting which leads it to love goodness for its own sake. All that is rational has this prompting. It never dies. It can never be entirely stifled. It may be darkened by the tempests and storms of guilt, but ever and anon the clouds roll away, and it shines out again. Murderers and thieves, and the most abandoned criminals, have been unable to deaden this faculty.

It came to be, that an hour arrived when the heart of the imprisoned fratricide held strange imagining. Old lessons and long forgotten hints, about heaven, and purity, and love, and gentle kindness, floated into his memory—vacillating, as it were, like delicate sea-flowers on the bosom of the turgid ocean. He remembered him of his brother as a boy—how they played together of the summer afternoons—and how, wearied out at evening, they slept pleasantly in each other's arms. O, Master of the Great Laws! couldst thou but roll back the years, and place that guilty creature a child again by the side of that brother! Such were the futile wishes of the criminal. And as repentance and prayer worked forth from his soul, he sank on the floor drowsily, and a tear stood beneath his eyelids.

Repentance and prayer from him! What hope could there be for aspirations having birth in a source so polluted? Yet the Sense which is never sleepless heard that tainted soul's desire, and willed that an answering mission should be sent straightway.

When Alza felt the mind of the Almighty in his heart—for it was rendered conscious to him in the moment—he cleaved the air with his swift pinions, and made haste to perform the cheerful duty. Along and earthward he flew—seeing far, far below him, mountains, and towns, and seas, and stretching forests. At distance, in the immeasurable field wherein he travelled, was the eternal glitter of countless worlds—wheeling and whirling, and motionless never. After a brief while the Spirit beheld the city of his destination; and, drawing nigh, he hovered over it—that great city, shrouded in the depths of night, and its many thousands slumbering.

Just as his presence, obedient to his desire, was transferring itself to the place where the murderer lay, he met one of his own kindred spreading his wings to rise from the ground.

"O Spirit," said Alza, "what a sad scene is here!"

"I grow faint," the other answered, "at looking abroad through these guilty places. Behold that street to the right."

He pointed, and Alza, turning, saw rooms of people, some with their minds maddened by intoxication, some uttering horrid blasphemies—sensual creatures, and wicked, and mockers of all holiness.

"O, brother," said the Tear-Angel, "let us not darken our eyes with the sight. Let us on to our appointed missions. What is yours, my brother?"

"Behold!" answered the Spirit.

And then Alza knew for the first time that there was a third living thing near by. With meek and abashed gesture, the soul of a girl just dead stood forth before them. Alza, without asking his companion, saw that the Spirit had been sent to guide and accompany the stranger through the Dark Windings.

So he kissed the brow of the re-born, and said,

"Be of good heart! Farewell, both!"

And the soul and its monitor departed upward, and Alza went into the dungeon.

Then, like a swinging vapor, the form of the Tear-Angel was by and over the body of the sleeping man. To his vision, night was as day, and day as night.

At first, something like a shudder went through him, for when one from the Pure Country approaches the wickedness of evil, the presence thereof is made known to him by an instinctive pain. Yet a moment, and the gentle Spirit cast glances of pity on the unconscious fratricide. In the great Mystery of Life, Alza remembered, though even he understood it not, it had been settled by the Unfathomable that Sin and Wrong should be. And the angel knew too, that Man, with all the darkness and the clouds about him, might not be contemned, even by the Princes of the Nighest Circle to the White Throne.

He slept. His hair, coarse and tangly through neglect, lay in masses about his head, and clustered over his neck. One arm was doubled under his cheek, and the other stretched straight forward. Long steady breaths, with a kind of hissing sound, came from his lips.

So he slumbered calmly. So the fires of a furnace, at night, though not extinguished, slumber calmly, when its swarthy ministers impel it not. Haply, he dreamed some innocent dream. Sleep on, dream on, outcast! There will soon be for you a reality harsh enough to make you wish those visions had continued alway, and you never awakened.

Oh, it is not well to look coldly and mercilessly on the bad done by our fellows. That convict—that being of the bloody hand—who could know what palliations there were for his guilt? Who might say there was no premature seducing aside from the walks of honesty—no seed of evil planted by others in his soul during the early years? Who should tell he was not so bred, that had he at manhood possessed aught but propensities for evil it would have been miraculous indeed? Who might dare cast the first stone?

The heart of man is a glorious temple; yet its Builder has seen fit to let it become, to a degree, like the Jewish structure of old, a mart for gross traffic, and the presence of unchaste things. In the Shrouded Volume, doubtless, it might be perceived how this is a part of the mighty and beautiful Harmony; but our eyes are mortal, and the film is over them.

The Angel of Tears bent him by the side of the prisoner's head. An instant more, and he rose, and seemed about to depart, as one whose desire had been attained. Wherefore does that pleasant look spread like a smile over the features of the slumberer?

In the darkness overhead yet linger the soft wings of Alza. Swaying above the prostrate mortal, the Spirit bends his white neck, and his face is shaded by the curls of his hair, which hang about him like a golden cloud. Shaking the beautiful tresses back, he stretches forth his hands, and raises his large eyes upward, and speaks murmuringly in the language used among the Creatures Beautiful:

"I come. Spirits of Pity and Love, favored children of the Loftiest—whose pleasant task it is with your pens of adamant to make record upon the Silver Leaves of those things which, when computed together at the Day of the End, are to outcancel the weight of the sum of evil—your chambers I seek!"

And the Angel of Tears glided away.

While a thousand air-forms, far and near, responded in the same tongue wherewith Alza had spoken:

"Beautiful, to the Eye of the Centre, is the sigh which ushers repentance!"

———

THE REFORMED.

* * * Mr. Marchion expressed his wonder at the strange and almost miraculous manner in which some persons, who appeared in the very deepest depth of the mire, would become reformed. A little trivial incident—an ordinary occurrence which seemed not worth the importance of a thought—would sometimes change the whole conduct of their wicked conduct, and present them to the world regenerated, and disenthralled. One instance, he said, had come to his knowledge in former times: which, if I felt disposed to hear it, he would relate.

I expressed my desire at the suggestion, and he commenced his narrative:

"Lift up!" was ejaculated as a signal—and click! went the glasses in the hands of a party of tipsey men, drinking one night at the bar of one of the middling order of taverns. And many a wild gibe was uttered, and many a terrible blasphemy, and many an impure phrase sounded out the pollution of the hearts of those half crazed creatures, as they tossed down their liquor, and made the walls echo with their uproar. The first and foremost in recklessness was a girlish-faced, fair-haired fellow of twenty-two or three years. They called him Mike. He seemed to be looked upon by the others as a sort of prompter, from whom they were to take cue. And if the brazen wickedness evinced by him in a hundred freaks and remarks to his companions, during their stay in that place, were any test of his capacity—there might be hardly one more fit to go forward as a guide on the road to destruction.

From the conversation of the party, it appeared that they had been spending the earlier part of the evening in a gambling house. The incidents spoken of as having occurred, and the conduct of Mike and his associates there, are not sufficiently tempting to be narrated.

A second, third and fourth time were the glasses filled, and the effect thereof began to be perceived in a still higher degree of noise and loquacity among the revellers. One of the serving-men came in at this moment, and whispered the bar-keeper, who went out, and in a moment returned again.

"A person," he said, "wished to speak with Mr. Michael. He waited on the walk in front."

The individual whose name was mentioned, made his excuse to the others, telling them he would be back in a moment, and left the room.— He had hardly shut the door behind him, and stepped into the open air, when he saw one of his brothers—his elder by eight or ten years—pacing to and fro with rapid and uneven steps. As the man turned in his walk, and the glare of the street lamp fell upon his face, the youth, half-benumbed as his own senses were, was somewhat startled at its paleness and perturbation.

"Come with me," said the elder brother, hurriedly, "the illness of our little Jane is worse, and I have been sent for you."

"Poh!" answered the young drunkard, very composedly, "is that all? I shall be home by-and-by."

And he turned to go back again.

"But brother, she is worse than ever before. Perhaps when you arrive she may be dead."

The tipsy one paused in his retreat, perhaps alarmed at the utterance of that dread word, which seldom fails to shoot a chill to the hearts of mortals. But he soon calmed himself, and waving his hand to the other:

"Why, see," said he, "a score of times, at least, have I been called away to the last sickness of our good little sister; and each time, it proves to be nothing worse than some whim of the nurse or the physician. Three years has the girl been able to live very heartily under her disease; and I'll be bound she'll stay on earth three years longer."

And as he concluded this wicked and most brutal reply, the speaker opened the door and went into the bar-room. But in his intoxication, during the hour that followed, Mike was far from being at ease. At the end of that hour, the words "perhaps when you arrive she may be dead," were not effaced from his hearing yet, and he started for home. The elder brother had wended his way back in sorrow.

Let me go before the younger one, awhile, to a room in that home. A little girl lay there dying. She was quite rational. She had been ill a long time; so it was no sudden thing for her parents, and her brethren and sisters, to be called for the solemn witness of the death agony.

The girl was not what might be called beautiful. And yet, there is a solemn kind of loveliness that always surrounds a sick child. The sympathy for the weak and helpless sufferer, perhaps, increases it in our ideas. The ashiness, and the moisture on the brow, and the film over the eye-balls—what man can look upon the sight and not feel his heart awed within him? Children, I have sometimes fancied too, increase in beauty as their illness deepens. The angels, it may be, are already vesting them with the garments they shall wear in the Pleasant Land.

Beside the nearest relatives of little Jane, standing round her bedside, was the family doctor. He had just laid her wrist down upon the coverlid, and the look he gave the mother, was a look in which there was no hope.

"My child!" she cried, in uncontrollable agony, "my child! you die!"

And the father, and the sons and daughters, were bowed down in grief, and thick tears rippled between the fingers held before their eyes.

Then there was silence awhile. During the hour just by-gone Jane had, in her childish way, bestowed a little gift upon each of her kindred, as a remembrance, when she should be dead and buried in the grave. And there was one of these simple tokens which had not reached its destination. She held it in her hand now. It was a very small, much-thumbed—a religious story for infants, given her by her mother when she had first learned to read.

While they were all keeping this solemn stillness—broken only by the suppressed sobs of those who stood and watched for the passing away of the girl's soul—a confusion of someone entering rudely and speaking in a turbulent voice, was heard in the adjoining apartment. Again the voice roughly sounded out; it was the voice of the drunkard Mike, and the father bade one of his sons go and quiet the intruder.

"If nought else will do," said he sternly, "put him forth by strength. We want no tipsy brawlers here, to disturb such a scene as this!"

For what moved the sick girl thus uneasily on her pillow, and raised her neck, and motioned to her mother? She would that Mike should be brought to her side. And it was enjoined on him whom the father had bade to eject the noisy one, that he should tell Mike his sister's request, and beg him to come to her.

He came. The inebriate—his mind sobered by the deep solemnity of the scene—stood there, and leaned over to catch the last accents of one who, in ten minutes more, was to be with the spirits of heaven.

All was the silence of deepest night. The dying child held the young man's hand in one of hers; with the other, she slowly lifted the trifling memorial she had assigned especially for him, aloft in the air. Her arm shook—her eyes, now becoming glassy with the death-damps, were cast toward her brother's face. She smiled pleasantly, and as an indistinct gurgle came from her throat, the uplifted hand fell suddenly into the open palm of her brother's, depositing the tiny volume there. Little Jane was dead.

From that night, the young man stepped no more in his wild courses, but was reformed.

When Mr. Marchion concluded his narrative, we sat some minutes in silence. I thought I noticed even more than usual interest concerning it, as he had drawn to its crisis—and I more half suspected he was himself the young man, whose reform had been brought about by the child's death. I was right. He acknowledged in answer to my questioning, that he had indeed been relating a story, the hero of which was himself.

———

LINGAVE'S TEMPTATION.

"Another day," uttered the poet Lingave, as he awoke in the morning, and turned him drowsily on his hard pallet, "another day comes out, burthened with its weight of woes. Of what use is existence to me? Crushed down beneath the merciless heel of Poverty, and no promise of hope to cheer me on, what have I in prospect but a life neglected, and a death of misery? "

The youth paused; but receiving no answer to his questions, thought proper to continue the peevish soliloquy without waiting any further.

"I am a genius, they say," and the speaker smiled bitterly, "but genius is not apparel and food. Why should I exist in the world, unknown, unloved, pressed with cares, while so many around me have all their souls can desire? I behold the splendid equipages roll by—I see the respectful bow at the presence of pride—and I curse the contrast between my own lot, and the fortune of the rich. The lofty air—the show of dress—the aristocratic demeanor—the glitter of jewels—dazzle my eyes; and sharp-toothed envy works within me. I hate these haughty and favored ones. Why: should my path be so much rougher than theirs? Pitiable, unfortunate man that I am! to be placed beneath those whom in my heart I despise—and to be constantly tantalized with the presence of that wealth I cannot enjoy!"

And the poet covered his eyes with his hands, and wept from very passion and fretfulness.

O, Lingave! be more of a man! Have you not the treasures of health and untainted propensities, which many of those you envy never enjoy? Are you not their superior in mental power, in liberal views of mankind, and in comprehensive intellect? And even allowing you the choice, how would you shudder at changing, in total, conditions with them? Besides, were you willing to devote all your time and energies, you could gain property too: squeeze, and toil, and worry, and twist everything into a matter of profit, and you can become a great man, as far as money goes to make greatness.

Retreat, then, Man of the Polished Soul, from those irritable complaints against your lot—those longings for wealth and puerile distinction, not worthy your class. Do justice, philosopher, to your own powers. While the world runs after its shadows and its bubbles, (thus commune in your own mind,) we will fold ourselves in our circle of understanding, and look with an eye of apathy on those things it considers so mighty and so enviable. Let the proud man pass with his pompous glance—let the gay flutter in finery—let the foolish enjoy his folly—and the beautiful move on in his perishing glory; we will gaze without desire on all their possessions and all their pleasures. Our destiny is different from theirs. Not for such as we, are the lowly flights of their crippled wings. We acknowledge no fellowship with them in ambition. We composedly look down on the paths where they walk, and pursue our own, without uttering a wish to descend, and be as they. What is it to us that the mass pay us not that deference which wealth commands? We desire no applause, save the applause of the good and the discriminating—the choice spirits among men. Our intellect would be sullied, were the vulgar to approximate to it, by professing to readily enter in, and praising it. Our pride is a towering, and a thrice refined pride.

When Lingave had given way to his temper some half hour, or thereabout, he grew more calm, and bethought himself that he was acting a very silly part. He listened a moment to the clatter of the carts, and the tramp of early passengers on the pave below, as they wended along to commence their daily toil. It was just ere sunrise, and the season was summer.

A little canary bird, the only pet poor Lingave could afford to keep, chirped merrily in its cage on the wall. How slight a circumstance will sometimes change the whole current of our thoughts! The music of that bird, abstracting the mind of the poet but a moment from his sorrows, gave a chance for his natural buoyancy to act again.

Lingave sprang lightly from his bed, performed his ablutions and his simple toilet in short order—then hanging the cage on a nail outside the window, and speaking an endearment to the songster, which brought a perfect flood of melody in return—he slowly passed through his door, descended the long narrow turnings of the stairs, and stood in the open street. Undetermined as to any particular destination, he folded his hands behind him, cast his glance upon the ground, and moved listlessly onward.

Hour after hour the poet walked along—up this street and down that—he recked not how or where. And as crowded thoroughfares are hardly the most fit places for a man to let his fancy soar in the clouds—many a push and shove and curse did the dreamer get bestowed upon him. The booming of the city clock sounded forth the hour twelve—high noon.

"Ho! Lingave!" cried a voice from an open basement window as the poet passed. He stopped, and then unwittingly would have walked on still, not fully awakened from his reverie.

"Lingave, I say!" cried the voice again, and the person to whom the voice attached, stretched his head quite out into the area in front, "stop, man. Have you forgotten your appointment?"

"Oh! ah!" said the poet, and he smiled unmeaningly, and descending the steps, went into the office of Ridman, whose call it was that had startled him in his walk.

Who was Ridman?—While the poet is waiting the convenience of that personage, it may be as well to explain.

Ridman was a money-maker. He had much penetration, considerable knowledge of the world, and a disposition to be constantly in the midst of enterprise, excitement, and stir. His schemes for gaining wealth were various; he had dipped into almost every branch and channel of business. A slight acquaintance of several years standing, subsisted between him and the poet. The day previous a boy had called with a note from Ridman to Lingave, desiring the presence of the latter at the money-maker's room. The poet returned for answer that he would be there. This was the engagement which he came near breaking.

Ridman had a smooth tongue. All his ingenuity was needed in the explanation to his companion of why and wherefore the latter had been sent for.

It is not requisite to state specifically the nature of the offer made by the man of wealth to the poet. Ridman, in one of his enterprises, found it necessary to procure the aid of such a person as Lingave—a writer of power, a master of elegant diction, of fine taste, in style passionate yet pure, and of the delicate imagery that belongs only to the Children of Song. The youth was absolutely startled at the magnificent and permanent remuneration which was held out to him for a moderate exercise of his talents.

But the nature of the services required! All the sophistry and art of Ridman could not veil its repulsiveness. The poet was to labor for the advancement of what he felt to be unholy—he was to inculcate what would lower the perfection of man. He promised to give an answer to the proposal the succeeding day, and left the place.

Now during the many hours there was a war going on in the heart of the poor poet. He was indeed poor; often, he had no certainty whether he should be able to procure the next day's meals. And the poet knew the beauty of truth, and adored, not in the abstract merely, but in practice, the excellence of upright principles.

Night came. Lingave, wearied, lay upon his pallet again and slept. The misty veil thrown over him, the Spirit of Poesy came to his visions, and stood beside him, and looked down pleasantly with her large eyes, which were bright and liquid like the reflection of stars in a lake.

Virtue, (such imagining, then, seemed conscious to the soul of the dreamer,) is ever the sinew of true genius. Together, the two in one, they are endowed with immortal strength, and approach loftily to Him from whom both spring.

Yet there are those that having great powers, bend them to the slavery of Wrong. God forgive them! for they surely do it ignorantly or heedlessly! Oh, could he who lightly tosses around him the seeds of evil, in his writings, or his enduring thoughts, or his chance words—could he see how, haply, they are to spring up in distant time and poison the air, and putrify and cause to sicken—would he not shrink back in horror! A bad principle, jestingly spoken—a falsehood, but of a word—may taint a whole nation!

Let the man to whom the Great Master has given the might of mind, beware how he uses that might. If for the furtherance of bad ends, what can be expected but that, as the hour of the closing scene draws nigh, thoughts of harm done and capacities distorted from their proper aim, and strength so laid out that men must be worse instead of better through the exertion of that strength—will come and swarm like spectres around him?

"Be and continue poor, young man," so taught one whose counsels should be graven on the heart of every youth, "while others around you grow rich by fraud and disloyalty. Be without place and power, while others beg their way upward. Bear the pain of disappointed hopes, while others gain the accomplishment of theirs by flattery. Forego the gracious pressure of a hand for which others cringe and crawl. Wrap yourself in your own virtue, and seek a friend and your daily bread. If you have, in such a course, grown gray with unblenched honor, bless God and die."

When Lingave awoke the next morning, there was no vacillating in his mind about the answer he should make to Ridman. He dispatched that answer, and then plodded on as in the days before.

———

THE MADMAN.

"Lo! See his eyeballs glare!" - Monk Lewis

The little tables of one of the large eating houses in the upper part of Fulton street, were crowded. It was an hour past noon. At that time, all classes of our citizens, except they who aspire to rank among the fashionable, or in the neighborhood of fashionable, either are engaged in the pleasant business of eating, or take measures for soon being so. The waiters, in their shirt sleeves, hurried to and fro, obeying the mandates of the customers. The carvers and cooks, at a little place partitioned off in a corner in the back part of the room, were tasked to their utmost. Knives and forks jingled, plates clattered, the names of the variety of dishes were sung out without a moments cessation.

It might have been noticed, by the curious eye, that nine out of ten who sought the accommodation there, gulped down their food with the most alarming haste, and in a manner which inferred that the crisis of some important transaction were just on the eve of happening—and its favorable conclusion depended on the celerity of mastication and swallowing. The large plain clock, at the top of the back wall, received many a hurried glance—as though the eaters timed themselves, and sought to get through the dining operations, within a given movement of the minute hands.

And there were two features which an observer might have noticed with great satisfaction. Each customer, upon finishing his meal, walked up to the counter and paid for it, according to his own computation—his own honesty being the only bar between a little petty cheating and the fair payment for what he had been served with. It is asserted that the instances of deception, from customers, are so rare as hardly to deserve mention. What a pleasant commentary on the attacks of foreign slanderers with respect to our national integrity! The second feature was the absence of any ardent liquors—no temptation existing for anyone to nullify the healthy action of the powers of the stomach upon what had been eaten, by drinking the unwholesome draught.

When the business and the confusion were at the highest, the door opened and admitted Richard Arden. Who was Richard Arden?

Anyone who has been familiar with life and people in a great city cannot have failed to notice a certain class, mostly composed of young men, who occupy a kind of medium between gentility and poverty. By soul, intelligence, manners, and a vague good taste, they assimilate to the former method. By irresolution of mind, evil acquaintances, a kind of romance which pervades the character, an incapacity for the harder and tougher and more profitable purposes of life, they attach to the latter.

Poverty, too, many times, is the source of much meanness. It causes the commission of a thousand things which result at last in the brushing off from the unfortunate poor one, of that fine sensitiveness which forms the most exquisite trait in the character of a true gentleman—that character which it ought to be our highest ambition to attain. I don't know, either, whether it may not be wrought out as well by a person surrounded with the disagreeables of want, and ill-breeding—as by one who has all the advantages of society and fashion. Let me make an impression in this passing remark, good reader.

Richard Arden had but fifteen cents in his pocket—and with that he intended to purchase his dinner. He had no certainty that he could get another meal afterward. Yet he was not cast down in spirit. He held his head well aloft. He bore upon his countenance the expression of one whose mind was but little agitated. He was a philosopher.

"Pork and beans, No. 8!" sung out Irish John, the waiter.

The words themselves may seem identified with anything in the world but refinement and romance. But they involve quite an amount of comfort, nevertheless. The smoking plate was brought—the crispy brown upon one side, and the rich fat slice of meat upon the other. Young Arden applied himself with great cheerfulness to the matter of devouring the savory viand.

What a hubbub! What a clatter of knives and forks!

One of the surest tests of good breeding is the manner of performing the little duties of meals and the table. A person whose fork dashes into the food before him, and whose knife divides it with the ferocity of a wild beast, has been unfortunate in his earlier education; and one remnant, at least, of the manners of a clown is still resident with him. Hurry is a vulgar trait, at best. At the table it becomes doubly so—inconsistent with health and prudence, as with decorum and enjoyment.

Our hero—for the reader has doubtless seen that the personage to whom he has been introduced is so—our hero was unexceptionable in the matter to which we have just alluded. Though in our establishment, and surrounded by companions, that would have shocked the fastidious delicacy of an Astor House boarder, or one whose dining hour was five or six o'clock, Arden comported himself with the quiet and deliberation which are at the root of good taste. So we think we have established for our principal character a claim to be considered a gentleman—an important point.

At the opposite side of the table sat a man of rather pleasant countenance, whom Arden had seen some few times previous, and with whom, on the present occasion, he happened to enter into some light talk.

As they discussed their dinner, they discussed one or two of the ordinary topics of conversation for some ten or fifteen minute.

How strangely we form acquaintances! How strange, indeed, and how complete a matter of chance, are many of those incidents and occurrences which have a lasting influence on a future destiny—trivial, as they seem at first, but potent for good or evil, in the future.

Arden and the pleasant-faced man, whose name was Barcoure, happened to get through their meal at the same time—to pay at the counter together—and to walk forth into the street together. Then they happened to be going a block or two in the same direction.

Why was it that they became acquaintances—and, are long, friends?

I cannot tell. At first they saw little or nothing—the one in the mind or manners of the other—to attract an admiration or respect in unwonted degree. Yet the next day, when they happened to meet, they bowed. The next day, each gave the other his name. The next week, they were on the footing of intimacy and familiarity.

―――

Barcoure was a young man—like my hero. Indeed it may be found, before the end of my story, that the right of main personage may lie between the two. He was of French descent—his father having come to America just after the downfall of the Napoleon dynasty, imbued with that fierce radicalism and contempt for religion which marked the old French revolution, and which still lingers among a by no means small portion of the people of that beautiful and noble country. The son inherited the sentiments, with the blood, of his father. His infidelity and his disregard of all the ties which custom and piety have established, more tempered with more discretion than his father had possessed—but they were none the less firm.

Perhaps I am not fully justifiable in calling Barcoure an infidel. He had ideas of morality and virtue, and, to a degree, practiced them. His system was a beautiful and a simple one—in theory—based upon a foundation of stern and strict and rigorous correctness of conduct. He rejected all of what he called the superstitions of mankind. He held that each code of religion contained more or less excellence—and more or less fanaticism. A strange and dreamy creature was Pierre Barcoure.

And before I advance any farther, it were well for me to remind the reader that I seek to paint life and men, in my narrative—describing them in such manner, and putting such words into their mouths, as may seem to make the portratures truthful ones. In what they say, I hold no responsibility.

To these two—Pierre and young Arden—became near and dear to one another.

Their friendship was not of that grosser kind which is rivetted by intimacy in scenes of dissipation. Many men in this great city of vice are banded together in a kind of companionship of vice, which they dignify by applying to it the word which stands second at the beginning of this paragraph. How vile a profanation of a holy term!

THE LOVE OF THE FOUR STUDENTS.

A CHRONICLE OF NEW-YORK.

O SUBTLE spirit, Love! in our earlier years, when the heart is fresh and the impulses strong, how potent your influence over us for good or for evil!1 The gyves wherewith you bind us, though softer and easier than silk, are firmer than bands of brass or iron. The sway of love over the mind of a man, though the old subject of flippant and sneering remarks from those who are too coarse to appreciate its delicate ascendancy, is a strange and beautiful thing.

Love! the mighty passion which, ever since human life began, has been conquering the great and subduing the humble, bending princes and mighty warriors, and the famous men of all nations, to the ground before it. Love! the delirious dream of youth, and the fond memory of old age. Love! which, with its canker-seed of decay within, has sent young men and maidens to a longed-for but too premature burial. Love! the child-monarch that death itself cannot overcome, but that has its tokens upon marble slabs at the head of grass-covered tombs; tokens more visible to the eye of the stranger, yet not so deeply graven as the face and the remembrances cut upon the heart of the living. Love! the sweet, the pure, the innocent; yet the causer of fierce hate, of wishes for deadly revenge, of bloody deeds, and madness, and the horrours of hell. Love! that wanders over battlefields, turning up mangled human trunks, and parting back the hair from gory faces, and daring the points of swords and the thunder of artillery, without a fear or a thought of danger.

New-York is my birth-place. My father was engaged in a moderate, respectable business, and we kept up a good appearance. Of my brothers and sisters I shall introduce only one, my brother Matthew, not quite two years younger than myself. He was a pleasant-looking but pale and delicate creature, and my mother often said that he was not long for this world. He had an inward affection, which troubled him in infancy, and which was never wholly eradicated. Mat, as we called him, was beloved by us all for his gentleness, amiability and singular quietness. He never was heard to complain of his illness, nor anything else; but there was still that gentle expression of the eye and the smile upon the lip, on any and every occasion when he spoke. My brother, however, was of keen sensitiveness, and had a tender heart beneath that calm exterior.

Well, time passed on. I was intended for the profession of the law; though, being lazy in my studies, it was not until my twenty-first year that I entered the office of an eminent practitioner, a rigid man, with whom I was to study and drudge.

The very first day of my appearance there, about the middle of the morning, there came to see my master a large, obtuse-looking woman, with a strong foreign accent. Her broken English, and a peculiar expression of the eye, excited the risibilities of a couple of young gentlemen, Mr. Harry Wheaton and Mr. Frank Brown, fellow-students of mine, and they commenced toward that lady what is called quizzing—a process which is generally the sure sign of a soft and pitiful brain in the originator.

I rebuked them, and, asking the woman into the adjoining room, sacred to our master's own use, I requested her to wait a few minutes and the lawyer would probably be there. With female tact, she made no allusion to the young men's impertinence, but thanked me with a dignity and politeness which I certainly did not at all expect. Before she went away that morning I found that she was a Swiss immigrant, a widow, and kept a little ale-house on the banks of the North river, at about two miles from what is now the centre of the city. Though the spot was then quite out of town, surrounded by trees and green fields, in these days it is well covered with buildings, and resounds to the clang of carts and the noise of traffic. The widow invited me, when I had a leisure afternoon, to come out and pay a visit to the ale-house; including in the invitation, alas! the other students—a piece of civility of which their rudeness had certainly not made them worthy.

It may not be amiss for me to describe more particularly my two companions in martyrdom—for that was the term which we unanimously voted as most applicable to the condition in which we were placed. Each was of the same age with myself. Wheaton was a handsome, red-cheeked, jovial fellow, full of mirth and spirits, and as generous and brave as any man I ever knew. He was very passionate, too; but the whirlwind of his temper was as quick in passing as it was violent, and, when over, unlike the whirlwinds, it left no desolation or wreck in its path. Frank Brown was a slim, tall, gracefully-formed youth, but by no means as handsome in the face as his companion. He was fond of vague metaphysical speculation, and used to fall in love regularly about once a month with any pretty girl he came across. The half of every Wednesday we had to ourselves, and, accompanied by my brother Matthew, who was studying under a French teacher in the same building, we were in the habit of having a sail, a ride, or a walk together.

One of those Wednesday afternoons, of a pleasant day in April, I bethought myself of the Swiss widow and her beer, about which latter article I had since her visit made inquiries, and heard spoken of in terms of high commendation. I mentioned the matter to Matthew, and to my brothers in martyrdom, and we agreed that there was no better way of filling up the hours than a visit. Accordingly we set forth, and, after a fine walk, arrived in glorious spirits at our destination.

Ah! how shall I describe the quiet beauties of the spot, with its long, low piazza looking out upon the river, and its clean, homely tables, and the tankards of real silver, in which the ale was given us, and the flavour of that excellent liquor itself. There was the fat Swiss widow, and there was a sober, stately old woman, half servant, half companion, Margery by name, and there was (good God! my fingers quiver yet as I write the name!) young Ninon, the daughter of the widow. O, through the years that have passed, my memory strays back, and that whole scene comes up before me again; and the brightest part of the picture is the strange ethereal beauty of that young girl! She was but sixteen, and the most fascinating, artless female I had ever beheld. She had soft blue eyes and light hair, and an expression of childish simplicity, which was charming to behold. I have no doubt that ere half an hour had elapsed from the time we entered the tavern, and saw Ninon, every one of the four of us, with the feelings of our age, loved the girl with the very depth of passion.

We neither spent as much or drank as much beer, by three-quarters, as we had intended before starting on the jaunt. The widow was very civil to us; and Margery, who waited upon us, though not quite a Hebe, behaved with a great deal of politeness; but it was to Ninon, after all, that the afternoon's pleasure was attributable; for, though we were strangers, we became acquainted at once, the manners of the girl, merry as she was, putting entirely out of view the most distant imputation of indecorum, and the presence of the widow and Margery (for we were all in the common room together, there being no other company) serving to make us all still more unembarrassed and at home. It was not till quite a while after sunset that we started on our return to our homes. We made several efforts to revive the fun and mirth which usually signalized our rambles when occasion allowed; but they seemed forced and discordant, like laughter in a sick room. Matthew was the only one who preserved his usual tenour of temper and conduct.

I need hardly say that thenceforward every Wednesday afternoon was spent by us at the widow's tavern. Strangely, neither Matthew, or my two fellow-students, or myself, spoke to each other of the sentiment which filled us, in reference to Ninon; yet we all knew the thoughts and feelings of the others; and each, perhaps, felt confident that his love alone was unsuspected by his companions.

The story of the widow was a simple yet touching one. In one of the cantons of her native land, she had grown up, and married, and lived in happy comfort. A son was born to her, and a daughter, the beautiful

Ninon. By some of those reverses of fortune which visit even those romantic and liberty-loving regions, the father and head of the family had the greater portion of his possessions swept from him. He struggled for a time against the evil influence, but it pressed upon him harder and harder. He had heard of a people in a western world—a new and swarming land, where the stranger was welcomed, and peace and the protection of the strong arm were around and over him. He had no heart to stay and struggle amid the scenes of his former being, and he determined to go, and make his home in that distant republic of the west. So, with his wife and children, and the proceeds of their little property, he took passage for New-York. Alas! he was never to reach his destination. Either the cares and troubles that preyed upon his mind, or some other cause, consigned him to a fit of illness, from which he was only relieved by the great dismisser from all griefs and agonies, Death. He was buried in the sea; and in due time his weeping family arrived at the great American emporium, to find that his death was only the first part of their deprivations. The son, he too sickened, and ere long was laid away to his rest.

Ninon was too young to feel permanent grief at these sad occurrences, and the mother, whatever she might have suffered inwardly, had a good deal of phelgm and patience, and set about making herself and her remaining child as comfortable as might be. They had still a respectable sum in cash, and, after due deliberation, the widow purchased the little quiet tavern, where, of Sundays and holydays, she took in considerable sums. The French and Germans visited the house frequently, and quite a number of young Americans, too. Probably, not the least attraction to the latter was the sweet face and form of Ninon.

Spring passed, and summer crept in and wasted away, and autumn had arrived. Every American knows what delicious weather we have, in these regions, of the early October days; how calm, clear, and divested of sultriness is the air, how blue the skies, and how decently nature seems preparing herself for her winter-sleep!

Thus it was of the Wednesday we started on our accustomed excursion. Six months had elapsed since our first visit, and, as then, we were full of the exuberance of young and joyful hearts. Frequent and hearty were our jokes, by no means particular about the theme or the method, and long and loud the peals of laughter that rang over the fields or along the shore.

We took our seats round the same clean white table, and received our liquor in the same bright tankards. They were set before us by the sober Margery, no one else being visible. As frequently happened, we were the only company. Walking and breathing the keen fine air had made us dry, and we soon drained the foaming vessels and called for more. I remember well an animated chat we had about some poems that had just made their appearance from a great British author, and were creating quite a sensation. There was one, a story of passion and despair, which Wheaton had read, and of which he gave us a transcript. It was a wild, startling, dreary thing, and perhaps it threw over our minds its peculiar cast.

An hour moved off, and we began to think it strange that neither Ninon or the widow came into the room. One of us gave a hint to that effect to Margery; but she made no answer, and went on with her usual way as before.

"The grim old thing," said Harry Wheaton; "if she were in Spain, they'd make her a premium duenna!"

I asked the woman about Ninon and the widow. She seemed perturbed, I thought; but, making no reply to the first part of my question, said that her mistress was in another room of the house, and did not wish to be with company.

"Then be kind enough," resumed Wheaton, with a grimace, "be kind enough, Mrs. Vinegar, to go and ask the widow if we can see Ninon."

Our attendant's face turned as pale as ashes, and she precipitately left the apartment. We laughed at her agitation, which Frank Brown (and we unanimously agreed thereto) assigned to her ill-temper at the ridicule of our company.

Quite a quarter of an hour elapsed before Margery's return. When she appeared, she told us briefly that the widow had bidden her obey our desire, and now, if we pleased, she would conduct us to the daughter's presence. There was a singular expression in the woman's eyes, and the whole affair began to strike us as somewhat odd; but we arose, and taking our caps, followed her as she stepped through the door. Back of the house were some fields, and our path leading into clumps of trees. At some thirty rods distant from the tavern, nigh one of these clumps, the largest tree whereof was a willow, Margery stopped, and pausing a minute, while we came up, spoke in tones calm and low:

"Ninon is there."

She pointed downward with her finger. Great God! there was a grave, new-made, and with the sods loosely joined, and a huge brown stone at each extremity! Some earth yet lay upon the grass nearby, and amid that whole scene our eyes took in nothing but that horrible, oven-shaped mound. My eyesight seemed to waver, my head felt dizzy, and a feeling of deadly nausea came over me. I heard a stifled exclamation, and looking round, saw Frank Brown fall heavily upon the grass in a fainting-fit. Wheaton gave way to his agony more fully than ever I had known a man before; he sobbed like a child, and wrung his hands. It is impossible to describe the suddenness and fearfulness of the sickening truth that came upon us all in such thunder-stroke force! Of all of us, my brother Matthew neither shed tears, or turned pale, or fainted, or gave any other evidence of inward depth of pain. His quiet, pleasant voice it was that recalled us, after the lapse of many long minutes, to ourselves.

So the girl had died and been buried. We were told, of a sudden illness that seized her the very day after our last preceding visit; but we inquired not into the particulars. The mother had that lucky toughness to sorrow which I have before alluded to, and outwardly seemed to grieve but little. For our own part, it was, perhaps, after all, not the depth of any intrinsic passion we shared toward Ninon, though we all loved her, but the startling, terrible way of the bursting upon us of the awful fact, which brought forth such abandonment to grief on the part of each of us, except my brother.

I come now to the conclusion of my story, and to the most curious part of it. The evening of the third day from our introduction to the girl's grave, Wheaton, who had wept scalding tears, and felt the perfect tempest of grief; and Brown, who had fallen as if stricken by a giant's club; and myself, that, for an hour, thought my heart would never rebound again from the fearful shock; that evening, I say, we three were seated around a table in another tavern, drinking other beer, and laughing as gleesomely as though we had never known the widow or her daughter—neither of whom, I venture to affirm, came into our minds once the whole night.

Strange are the contradictions of the things of life! The seventh day after that dreadful visit saw my brother Matthew, him who, alone of all the four, had been cold to the breath of the withering blast; the weak and delicate one, who, while bold men and brave men writhed in torture or lay stunned upon the ground, had kept the same placid, gentle face, and the same untrembling fingers; the one who complained not, raved not, recurred not to the subject; him that seventh day saw a clay-cold corpse, shrouded in the pale cerements of decay, and carried to the repose of the churchyard and the coffin. The malignant shaft, far, far down and within, wrought a poison and a pain too great for show, and the youth died.

———

ERIS; A SPIRIT RECORD.

WHO says that there are not angels or invisible spirits watching around us? The teeming regions of the air swarm with bodiless ghosts—bodiless to human sight, because of their exceeding and too dazzling beauty!

And there is one, childlike, with helpless and unsteady movements, but a countenance of immortal bloom, whose long-lashed eyes droop downward. The name of the shape is Dai. When he comes near, the angels are silent, and gaze upon him with pity and affection. And the fair eyes of the shape roll, but fix upon no object; while his lips move, but a plaintive tone only is heard, the speaking of a single name. Wandering in the confines of earth, or restlessly amid the streets of the beautiful land, goes Dai, earnestly calling on one he loves.

Wherefore is there no response?

Soft as the feathery leaf of the frailest flower—pure as the heart of flame—of a beauty so lustrous that the sons of Heaven themselves might well be drunken to gaze thereon—with fleecy robes that but half apparel a maddening whiteness and grace—dwells Eris among the creatures beautiful, a chosen and cherished one. And Eris is the name called by the wandering angel,—while no answer comes, and the loved flies swiftly away, with a look of sadness and displeasure.

It had been years before that a maid and her betrothed lived in one of the pleasant places of earth. Their hearts clung to each other with the fondness of young life, and all its dreamy passion. Each was simple and innocent. Mortality might not know a thing better than their love, or more sunny than their happiness.

In the method of the rule of fate, it was ordered that the maid should sicken, and be drawn nigh to the gates of death—nigh, but not through them. Now to the young who love purely, High Power commissions to each a gentle guardian, who hovers around unseen day and night. The office of this spirit is to keep a sleepless watch, and fill the heart of his charge with strange and mysterious and lovely thoughts. Over the maid was placed Dai, and through her illness the unknown presence of the youth hung near continually.

To the immortal, days, years and centuries are the same.

Erewhile, a cloud was seen in Heaven. The delicate ones bent their necks, and shook as if a chill blast had swept by—and white robes were drawn around shivering and terrified forms.

An archangel with veiled cheeks cleaved the air. Silence spread through the hosts of the passed away, who gazed in wonder and fear. And as they gazed they saw a new companion of wondrous loveliness among them—a strange and timid creature, who, were it not that pain must never enter those borders with innocence, would have been called unhappy. The angels gathered around the late comer with caresses and kisses, and they smiled pleasantly with joy in each other's eyes.

Then the archangel's voice was heard—and they who heard it knew that One still mightier spake his will therein:

"The child Dai!" said he.

A far reply sounded out in tones of trembling and apprehension,

"I am here!"

And the youth came forth from the distant confines, whither he had been in solitude. The placid look of peace no more illumined his brow with silver light, and his unearthly beauty was as a choice statue enveloped in mist and smoke.

"Oh, weak and wicked spirit!" said the archangel, "thou hast been false to thy mission and thy Master!"

The quivering limbs of Dai felt weak and cold. He would have made an answer in agony—but at that moment he lifted his eyes and beheld the countenance of Eris, the late comer.

Love is potent, even in Heaven! And subtle passion creeps into the hearts of the sons of beauty, who feel the delicious impulse, and know that there is a soft sadness sweeter than aught in the round of their pleasure eternal.

When the youth saw Eris, he sprang forward with lightning swiftness to her side. But the late comer turned away with aversion. The band of good-will might not be between them, because of wrongs done, and the planting of despair in two happy human hearts.

At the same moment, the myriads of interlinked spirits that range step by step from the throne of the Uppermost, (as the power of that light and presence which is unbearable even to the deathless, must be tempered for the sight of any created thing, however lofty,) were conscious of a motion of the mind of God. Quicker than electric thought the command was accomplished! The disobedient angel felt himself enveloped in a sudden cloud, impenetrably dark. The face of Eris gladdened and maddened him no more. He turned himself to and fro, and stretched out his arms—but though he knew the nearness of his companions, the light of Heaven, and of the eyes of Eris, was strangely sealed to him. The youth was blind forever.

So a wandering angel sweeps through space with restless and unsteady movements—and the sound heard from his lips is the calling of a single name. But the loved flies swiftly away in sadness, and heeds him not. Onward and onward speeds the angel, amid scenes of ineffable splendor, though to his sight the splendor is darkness. But there is one scene that rests before him always. It is of a low brown dwelling among the children of men; and in an inner room a couch, whereon lies a young maid, whose cheeks rival the frailness and paleness of foam. Nearby is a youth; and the filmy eyes of the girl are bent upon him in fondness. What dim shape hovers overhead? He is invisible to mortals; but oh! well may the blind spirit, by the token of throbs of guilty and fiery love beating through him, know that hovering form! Thrust forward by such fiery love, the shape dared transcend his duty. Again the youth looked upon the couch, and beheld a lifeless corpse.

This is the picture upon the vision of Dai. His brethren of the bands of light, as they meet him in his journeyings, pause awhile for pity; yet never do the pangs of their sympathy, the only pangs known to those sinless creatures, or arms thrown softly around him, or kisses on his brow, efface the pale lineaments of the sick girl—the dead.

In the portals of Heaven stands Eris, oft peering into the outer distance. Nor of the millions of winged messengers that hourly come and go, does one enter there whose features are not earnestly scanned by the watcher. And the fond joy resides in her soul, that the time is nigh at hand; for a thread yet binds the angel down to the old abode, and until the breaking of that bond, Eris keeps vigil in the portals of Heaven.

The limit of the watch comes soon. On earth, a toil-worn man has returned from distant travel, and lays him down, weary and faint at heart, on a floor amid the ruins of that low brown dwelling. The slight echo is heard of moans coming from the breast of one who yearns to die. Life, and rosy light, and the pleasant things of nature, and the voice and sight of his fellows, and the glory of thought—the sun, the flowers, the glittering stars, the soft breeze—have no joy for him. And the coffin and the cold earth have no horror; they are a path to the unforgotten.

Thus the tale is told in Heaven, how the pure love of two human beings is a sacred thing, which the immortal themselves must not dare to cross. In pity to the disobedient angel he is blind, that he may not gaze ceaselessly on one who returns his love with displeasure. And haply Dai is the spirit of the destiny of those whose selfishness would seek to mar the peace of gentle hearts, by their own unreturned and unhallowed passion.

———

MY BOYS AND GIRLS.

THOUGH a bachelor, I have several girls and boys that I consider my own. Little Louisa, the fairest and most delicate of human blossoms, is a lovely niece—a child that the angels themselves might take to the beautiful land, without tasting death. A fat, hearty, rosy-cheeked youngster, the girl's brother, comes in also for a good share of my affection. Never was there such an imp of mischief! Falls and bumps hath he every hour of the day, which affect him not, however. Incessant work occupies his mornings, noons and nights; and dangerous is it, in the room with him, to leave anything unguarded, which the most persevering activity of a stout pair of dumpy hands can destroy.

What would you say, dear reader, were I to claim the nearest relationship to George Washington, Thomas Jefferson and Andrew Jackson? Yet such is the case, as I aver upon my word. Several times has the immortal Washington sat on my shoulders, his legs dangling down upon my breast, while I trotted for sport down a lane or over the fields. Around the waist of the sagacious Jefferson have I circled one arm, while the fingers of the other have pointed him out words to spell. And though Jackson is (strange paradox!) considerably older than the other two, many a race and tumble have I had with him—and at this moment I question whether, in a wrestle, he would not get the better of me, and put me flat.

One of my children—a child of light and loveliness—sometimes gives me rise to many uneasy feelings. She is a very beautiful girl, in her fourteenth year. Flattery comes too often to her ears. From the depths of her soul I now and then see misty revealings of thought and wish, that are not well. I see them through her eyes and in the expression of her face.

It is a dreary thought to imagine what may happen, in the future years, to a handsome, merry child—to gaze far down the vista, and see the dim phantoms of Evil standing about with nets and temptations—to witness, in the perspective, purity gone, and the freshness of youthful innocence rubbed off, like the wasted bloom of flowers. Who, at twenty-five or thirty years of age, is without many memories of wrongs done, and mean or wicked deeds performed?

Right well do I love many more of my children. H. is my "summer child." An affectionate fellow is he—with merits and with faults, as all boys have—and it has come to be that should his voice no more salute my ears, nor his face my eyes, I might not feel as happy as I am. M., too, a volatile lively young gentleman, is an acquaintance by no means unpleasant to have by my side. Perhaps M. is a little too rattlesome, but he has qualities which have endeared him to me much during our brief acquaintance. Then there is J. H., a sober, good-natured youth, whom I hope I shall always number among my friends. Another H. has lately come among us—too large, perhaps, and too near manhood, to be called one of my children. I know I shall love him well when we become better acquainted—as I hope we are destined to be.

Blessings on the young! And for those whom I have mentioned in the past lines, oh, may the developement of their existence be spared any sharp stings of grief or pangs of remorse! Had I any magic or superhuman power, one of the first means of its use would be to insure the brightness and beauty of their lives. Alas! that there should be sin, and pain, and agony so abundantly in the world!—that these young creatures—wild, frolocksome, and fair—so dear to me all of them, those connected by blood, and those whom I like for themselves alone—alas, that they should merge in manhood and womanhood the fragrance and purity of their youth!

But shall I forget to mention one other of my children? For of him I can speak with mingled joy and sadness. For him there is no fear in the future. The clouds shall not darken over his young head—nor the taint of wickedness corrupt his heart—nor any poignant remorse knaw him inwardly for wrongs done. No weary bane of body or soul—no disappointed hope—no unrequited love—no feverish ambition—no revenge, nor hate, nor pride—no struggling with poverty, nor temptation, nor death—may ever trouble him more. He lies low in the grave-yard on the hill. Very beautiful was he—and the promise of an honorable manhood shone brightly in him—and sad was the gloom of his passing away. We buried him in the early summer. The scent of the apple-blossoms was thick in the air—and all animated nature seemed overflowing with delight and motion. But the fragrance and the animation made us feel a deadlier sickness in our souls. Oh, bitter day! I pray God there may come to me but few such!

And there is one again:—and she, too, must be in the Land of Light, so tiny and so frail. A mere month only after she came into the world, a little shroud was prepared, and a little coffin built, and they placed the young infant in her tomb. It was not a sad thing—we wept not, nor were our hearts heavy.

I bless God that he has ordained the beautiful youth and spring time! In all the wondrous harmony of nature, nothing shows more wisdom and benevolence than that necessity which makes us grow up from so weak and helpless a being as a new-born infant, through all the phases of sooner and later childhood, to the neighborhood of maturity, and so to maturity itself. Thus comes the sweetness of the early seasons—the bud and blossom time of life. Thus comes the beauty which we love to look upon—the faces and lithe forms of young children.

May it not be well, as we grow old, to make ourselves often fresh, and childlike, and merry with those who are so fresh and merry? We must grow old—for immutable time will have it so. Gray hairs will be sown in our heads, and wrinkles in our faces; but we can yet keep the within cheerful and youthful—and that is the great secret of warding off all that is unenviable in old age. The fountain flowing in its sweetness forever, and the bloom undying upon the heart, and the thoughts young, whatever the body may be—we can bid defiance to the assaults of time, and composedly wait for the hour of our taking away.

THE FIREMAN'S DREAM.

WITH THE STORY OF HIS STRANGE COMPANION.
A TALE OF FANTASIE.

"'Twas in the fitful fashion of a dream."
   -Grenville Mellen, *Dream of the Sea*

Chapter I.

*"Young he was and vigorous,
And just on the third seventh of his age—
With many virtues and some vices too,
But both such as we love. Indeed my liege,
An excellent man of a most excellent class."*
                      —Old Play

"What shall I do with myself to-day?" was the thought that first sprang in the mind of a young New Yorker, as he awoke and turned over in bed some time after day light, one morning last summer. The bed was in an attic room of a house in one of those thoroughfares that run down from Division street to Houston. A window opened to the eastward, and George Willis, the occupant of the bed, lazily gazing out of it, saw that the prospect was fair for a most beautiful day. The eastern horizon was just lighting up with the beams of the sun, whose broad face had already appeared. The immense expanse of brick, the stacks of chimneys, and the far stretching streets, were tipped with the golden beams—and as the young man gazed, he felt that pleasant and agreeable sensation which results from having a good stock of health and animal spirits, refreshed by a night's wholesome sleep, and no cares pressing on the mind. He rose, and leisurely proceeded to make himself ready for breakfast.

It may not be amiss here to occupy the time which George takes in dressing, to tell who and what he is. The house of which the bedroom in the attic story was part, was owned by a respectable and industrious cabinet maker, and "our hero" (as the tale-writers say) was one of his apprentices. Two months more would make the young man of age—when, as the probabilities were, he would be installed in a profitable situation in his master's establishment, mutually to the satisfaction of the employer and the employed.

Young Willis was an agreeable fellow, whom everybody liked;—and if he had any foible in the world it was a surpassing love and fondness for his "machine," as he called the fire-engine he had attached himself to. For he was one of that noble class of which New York ought to be proud, the firemen. Nor is it any drawback upon the merit of the really gallant and deserving ones of the body we mention, that there are some scoundrels among them. Amid a class so large and mixed, it would be impossible to have all perfect. The wonder is, that the number of the vicious is not greater than it really is.

At breakfast, George made up his mind that about as pleasant a way of spending his Sunday as any he could think of, would be by an excursion to Hoboken. He announced his intention to some of the other male members of the family, and was soon furnished with several companions.

For the purposes of our story, it is not necessary to follow the young fireman and his friends, in all their sayings and doings during the jaunt. That they were delighted is a matter of course—for who could go over to Hoboken, of a pleasant summer day and not be delighted?

One of the principal incidents of the afternoon was the sight of, and conversation with, a party of Indians, a dozen or more in number, who had three small tents under the spreading branches of some of the trees, and who appeared to be an object of considerable curiosity to all the spectators. There was one of the more youthful portion of these Indians, a man of about twenty three or four, that attracted more than ordinary attention. Willis and his party were pleased with him, and invited him to partake of some small refreshment with them. They sat and chatted with the young savage for an hour or more. He told them many anecdotes of forest customs, and of his own life—and it was almost with regret that the middle of the afternoon made it necessary for the party to leave their new acquaintance and return to New York.

The evening was as beautiful as the day had been. George sat at a window at the back of the house looking out into quite a handsome garden which covered the yard owned by the cabinet maker. He was somewhat tired and exhausted by the amusements of the day, and had just made up his mind to retire uncommonly early to bed, when his ears were saluted by a sound which never fails to put every New York fireman on the alert.

Clang! clang! clang! went the great bell of the City Hall. And with a lesser loudness, but quite as much activity, soon followed a whole host of other bells.

Nothing surprises strangers in New York more than the sudden life and readiness for action, evinced by the city firemen, the moment the warning notes of danger are flung forth upon the breeze. The echoes of the first stroke have hardly died away, when hundreds of men with their pilot cloth coats, and ponderous black fire-caps, are seen sallying along, with might and main, in the direction of the burning tenement.

On this occasion the fire was in the neighborhood of the Park. The up-town engines, were close on the heels of their down-town competitors, and though the flames had made considerable headway, all hands immediately commenced taking the most active means for arresting their progress. Ladders were quickly placed in such positions as were necessary to enable them to pull down certain portions connecting the burning parts with others as yet uninjured—and ropes and huge hooks, were applied to the half consumed beams—which soon brought them to the ground.

Who so active and enthusiastic in the whole affair as George Willis? But alas! the ungrateful fate that too often rewards efforts of heroic daring—a daring not seldom met with among the New York firemen—was destined to fall to no slight extent here. An immense portion of the roof and side, though not in a burning state itself had been undermined, and its support withdrawn, by the progress of the flames beneath, and suddenly fell on the heads of a number of the most venturesome of the firemen. One man was instantly killed. Several were burnt—and George was struck to the earth, apparently lifeless, by a tremendous blow on his head. No sooner however had the involuntary exclamations of horror caused by the sight of the falling timbers burst from the spectators' lips, than prompt means were taken to aid the sufferers and obviate the damage as far as could be. A thousand willing forms and brave hands pressed forward to drag the stricken down bodies of their comrades from their perilous situation. It was at first thought that George Willis was dead; but closer examination proved that he had only received a severe wound on the head, which, however dangerous, had not as yet deprived him of life.

By the assistance and direction of some young friends, who fortunately were nigh at hand, he was forthwith taken to his own home, and received every attention that the kindest affection on the part of the cabinet maker's wife, and a good looking girl, the daughter, could procure.

Behold our young firemen, then, lying on the bed from which he had risen so comfortably in the morning, senseless and with an ugly gash just over his forehead. He soon found his faculties of speech, it is true, but they were only used to give utterance to the most vague fantasies of a brain fever, which now set in. The poor fellow knew none of those about him. He imagined himself in the trackless Indian forests of the west, and talked incessantly in the most wild and dreamy manner.

The physician who was sent for prescribed some medicines which, after a short time, had a soothing effect, and the youth sunk into a comparatively quiet sleep. But though outwardly calm, his volatile and active mind partook of the restlessness of those brains, where "reason's lord sits lightly on his throne," and vibrated to and fro apparently without direction or point.

Poor George wandered awhile, (as he afterwards related to the family), amid such unearthly scenes of tumult, as were never before imagined by mortal man. The heated rays of the sun shown down upon him, with the most painful and relentless fury, and it seemed as though his blood was simmering in his veins. Immense sounds as of the booming of mighty bells kept throbbing in his ears and he was hurried forward, by the force of a resistless crowd.

Now there was a fire company towards which the one George belonged to, had a bitter feeling. This bitterness had never proceeded to any length beyond sharp words; but it was sadly feared some occasion might arise which would lead to one of those sanguinary riots which are the saddest disgrace to the firemen of New York—though in this respect, New York does not approach the doings of a certain sister city not a hundred miles off.

As George was walking, he himself could not exactly tell where, he was sneeringly accosted by a man whom he knew to be a member of the detested company. A reply of severity was returned—and then commenced a war of words, which grew hotter and hotter on either side, until neither party could contain the worked up ferocity of his nature. They made for each other, and clenched in a deadly grapple.

For some minutes, as they rolled over upon the ground, victory seemed in doubt. But in one of the turnings, George came uppermost, and with one of his arms free. Quick as lightning he drew a knife from his breast and plunged it into the other's heart. A second and a third plunge completed the work of death, and then the bleeding corpse of a fellow creature lay before the young fireman, stiffening in its own clotted gore. It was most horrible!

Need we add that the awful reality of such a dream has more than once occurred in our city?

It would be impossible to transcribe all the capricious incidents and adventures of the sick man. After a while, however, they began to be reduced to more method. He was walking and gazing in a wilderness far from the abodes of civilized beings. Through the trees he occasionally caught glimpses of a majestic river; on the opposite bank of which he once saw a group of deer-skin huts, and nigh at hand the forms of some dusky children, at play. By his side was a companion, not much beyond his own age, but of the hue of the sons of the forest. The heat was overpowering; and as they came out by a grassy knoll in the wood, in the centre of which was a bubbling brook of clear water, they agreed to throw themselves down, and rest awhile there. And the companion, at the request of the young man, began to while away the time with talk.—He told the story of his own life. He mourned over the decay of his ancient race;—and the fires that once or twice flashed from his eyes proved, that, had a fit opportunity offered, he would have shown himself no cowardly scion of their warlike stock. Yet he had a gentle manner, and a soft winning voice—and the ears of the listener drank in his narrative with delight.

Chapter II.

STORY OF THE FIREMAN'S STRANGE COMPANION.

The blackbird is singing on Michigan's shore
As sweetly and wildly as ever before.
The sun looks as ruddy and rises as bright,
And reflects oe'r the waters as beamy a light;
Each bird and each beast it is blessed in degree
All nature is cheerful, all happy but me.
                    - Henry Rowe Schoolcraft, Geehale

I am a white man by education and an Indian by birth. Within my bosom reside two opposing elements, which ever refuse to mix with one another, and often war fiercely, and rack my soul with great pain. These elements are the influences of my nature on the one side, and those of my habits on the other. Let me tell you how I came among your people.

Far in the outskirts of one of the Western States, lived a hardy pioneer, and his quite as hardy wife. Of the two, she possessed much the more bold and masculine disposition. She hunted with him in the forest—caught fish in the stream—and felled trees to clear the land, with her own arms. The name of this couple was Boane—hers, Violet—his, Sampson. She was tall and large-limbed, with brawny hands, and coarse features; but good nature and kindness dwelt upon those features, and she had a merry and gentle heart in that huge wall of flesh. Her husband might have been about half her size and weight—he was a little, abject, obedient creature, and never entertained much opinion of his own. He had one son, a youth of twenty, who partook more of the mother than the father—being mighty in size, like her, and also merry in soul. In the east, where they lived previous to their emigration, Harry Boane sailed in a coasting vessel as a mariner. He was fond of the water and always retained the garb of the craft.

The gentle Violet and her son would frequently recreate themselves with a sail upon the river which passed the door of their log-cabin, and emptied into a branch of the great Mississippi, hundreds of miles away. Sometimes they journeyed several miles up the stream, where there was a favorite spot for fishing. It was on one of these occasions that my fortunes happened to be interlinked with theirs. Thus it was:

Evening had began to sprinkle her hue of gloom on the trees and the river. The wild-fowl were seeking their marshy nests—and the prairie fox looked forth from his burrow to see how long ere he might saunter abroad for plunder. Violet and her son were floating idly along the current of the river, in their boat, toward home. She had the helm, and he was rowing, though with little outlay of strength.

As they pushed by the overhanging shrubbery of a part of the shore, all of a sudden a sharp and prolonged cry struck their ears. It was as from a human being in distress. They were startled, and instinctively pushed out into the stream. They had heard of the tricks of the cunning savages to lure the whites to destruction; and were somewhat superstitious withal.

Not many moments elapsed before the cry sounded again upon the cool evening breeze—and they felt sure that it was no deception. It was that cry—what mother's ear ever failed her to tell it correctly? the cry of a young child. It rose long and wailing again—a piteous cry—bearing in its tones an entreaty to all charatable hearts for succor and protection.

"Pull to the shore," commanded the woman, at once.

Harry obeyed—and a couple of vigorous thrusts of his boat-pole impelled the tiny vessel in the midst of the bog and brambles that lined the margin of the stream. They jumped upon land.

Guided by the moaning accents, which now pierced the air with redoubled loudness, they soon came out upon a little opening, either artificial or left so by nature, some three or four rods from the shore. There, upon the ground, without mat or couch other than the leaves, lay an Indian child—a boy of six or seven years. He made many signs of agony, and upon their bending over him, he pointed with gestures which though mute they could not fail of comprehending to one of his ankles. It was badly sprained. The least motion was like probing the very marrow of the bones.

The child was perfectly naked. He had no covering, not even the skin of a wild beast. He spoke not, unless a rough and unintelligible exclamation, consisting of two syllables only, repeated over and over again, might be called speaking. Literally, he seemed a wild and untamed creature, a companion of the forest bears—and abandoned by his own species.

Never did the gentle Violet look upon anything in the shape of tangible misery, which act of hers could relieve, without doing her best for effecting that relief. With as much tenderness as possible, she and Harry conveyed the boy to the boat, and bestowed him there in the easiest posture. He seemed sensible of their kindness, and repaid it by grateful glances of his round black eyes.

The journey home was made with as much speed as the situation of things would admit. Arrived there, the kindness of Violet did not pause at any attentions or motherly nursings. She bandaged the foot of the poor Indian boy with soothing balsams, and placed him on a soft and easy couch, and gave him cooling refreshments. He could not talk to her—for he knew no language of the mouth. But the gratitude of those black eyes was a hundred times stronger.

That Indian boy was myself.

I will be asked in vain to explain the method of my being wounded in the forest that evening—and why I was there alone. As I struggle sometimes to carry my memory back, and account for the preceding events, all is like a dark and ill dream, leaving a hateful recollection upon the mind, but the nature and the details of which I cannot comprehend. I know not whether I was lost from some wandering family—or whether I was abandoned by an inhuman parent. Sometimes I think that my tribe might have been destroyed in war, either with the whites or with people of their own color, and I, accidentally left for dead in the midst of my kindred's corpes, rose and wandered through the forest in my infant helplessness, and yet was preserved by the hand of the Great Spirit, whose eye loses not sight even of orphans in the untravelled wild. What miracle led to my continued life, exposed to the rigor of the seasons, and without shelter—be this latter supposition correct—it is impossible for me to say. Did the berries and the nuts afford me food? Found I a bed in the vacated lair of some forest panther? Gamboled I with the wild squirrels, or played with the young cubs? To this day I can climb the hugest tree or the lithest sapling as nimbly as a cat frightened by schoolboys.

Violet and her people were very kind to me. I was clothed by them, and in a few days when my hurt was healed, and I went forth and saw how they lived, and heard the sound of their voices to one another—that mystery of conveyance of thoughts which I could not understand—a strange revolution took place within me. They told me with smiles to stay with them, and be their son. My eyes answered, yes.

So I learned language. I can remember even now the infantile curiosity with which I would take various articles to Violet and sign to her an inquiry for their names—and when she uttered them how I would try to pronounce them myself—and what mistakes I made—and how her loud laugh would jingle forth at the comical method of those mistakes—and how I myself would join in the laugh, and then try again, and at last succeed.

I became soon the very pet of all of them, and necessary to their happiness. Violet loved me, and Harry jestingly called me his little son.

Boane, the husband, I cared not so much for; my nature assimilated to the bold the manly and the strong. Yet, I believe, I was ever gentle, and easily led.

They, in the course of time when their neighborhood was more thickly populated, and a school was established, sent me to learn the various branches of education. I soon outstripped my fellows, and was noted for the most studious of all the pupils. Only one of them came near to me, in my progress. This was my playfellow Anthony Clark, a distant relative of the Boanes, an orphan like myself, and of about my own age.

Anthony Clark, my young competitor at school, had come to live with Boanes, (why should I not have mentioned this before, when the name of the person is burnt in welcome characters of fire upon my soul?) a few seasons after I was found so strangely in the forest. He was from the east—and came out with one of the bands of emigrants.

———

DUMB KATE. - An Early Death

NOT many years since—and yet long enough to have been before the abundance of railroads, and similar speedy modes of conveyance—the travellers from Amboy village to the metropolis of our republic were permitted to refresh themselves, and the horses of the stage had a breathing spell, at a certain old-fashioned tavern, about half way between the two places. It was a quaint, comfortable, ancient house, that tavern. Huge buttonwood trees embowered it round about, and there was a long porch in front, the trellised work whereof, though old and mouldered, had been, and promised still to be for years, held together by the tangled folds of a grape vine wreathed about it like a tremendous serpent.

How clean and fragrant everything was there! How bright the pewter tankards wherefrom cider or ale rolled through the lips into the parched throat of the thirsty man! How pleasing to look into the expressive eyes of Kate, the landlord's lovely daughter, who kept everything so clean and bright!

Now the reason why Kate's eyes had become so expressive was, that, besides their proper and natural office, they stood to the poor girl in the place of tongue and ears also. Kate had been dumb from her birth.

Everybody loved the helpless creature when she was a child. Gentle, timid, and affectionate was she, and delicately beautiful as the lilies of which she loved to cultivate so many every summer in her garden. Her brown hair, and the like-colored lashes, so long and silky, that drooped over her blue eyes of such uncommon size and softness—her rounded shape, well set off by a little modest art of dress—her smile—the graceful ease of her motions, always attracted the admiration of the strangers who stopped there, and were quite a pride to her parents and friends.

Dumb Kate had an education which rarely falls to the lot of a country girl. She had been early taught to read, and notwithstanding her infirmity, had most of those accomplishments which usually fall to the lot of the daughters of wealth and prosperity.

How could it happen that so innocent and beautiful and inoffensive a being was made to taste, even to its dregs, the bitter cup of unhappiness? Oh, there must indeed be a mysterious, unfathomable meaning in the decrees of Providence, which is beyond the comprehension of man; for no one on earth less deserved or needed "the uses of adversity" than Dumb Kate.

Love, the mighty and lawless passion, came into the sanctuary of the maid's pure breast, and the dove of peace fled away forever. What heart, what situation in life is superior to love? Even this young country girl, retired from the busier and more exciting scenes of existence, was made to know the sweet intoxication, as well as the madness, that comes with the attacks of that boy-conqueror.

One of the persons who had occasion to stop most frequently at the tavern kept by Dumb Kate's parents was a young man, the son of a gentleman farmer, who owned a handsome estate in the neighborhood. He saw Kate, and was struck with her beauty and natural elegance. Though not of thoroughly wicked propensities, the merit of so fine a prize made this man determine, without intending marriage, to gain her love, and if possible, to win her to himself. At first he hardly dared, even to his own soul, to entertain thoughts of vileness or harm against one so confiding and childlike. But in a short time such feelings wore away, and he made up his mind to become the betrayer of poor Kate.

As the girl's evil genius would have it, the youth was handsome and of most pleasing address. He laid his plans with the greatest art. The efforts of wickedness triumphed. It is needless to transcribe the progress of this devil in angel's guise. He had made but too sure of his victim. Kate was lost!

Look not with a frown, rigid moralist! Give not words and thoughts of contempt, you whose life has been pure because it has never been tempted, or because you had the wisdom of the serpent to resist temptation! There is an Eye which looks far beneath the surface of conduct, and forgives and pities the infirmities of mortal weakness. To that Eye, it not seldom appears that they upon whom the world has placed its ban, are the fittest for entering the abodes of heaven itself—while others, to whom men look up with reverence and admiration, might make their appropriate home amid spirits of darkness.

The successful villain came to New York soon after, and engaged in a respectable business which prospered well, and which has no doubt by this time made him what is called a man of fortune.

Not long did sickness of the heart wear into the life and happiness of Dumb Kate. One pleasant spring day, the neighbors having been called by a notice the previous morning, the old church-yard was thrown open, and a coffin was borne over the early grass that seemd so delicate with its light green hue. There was a new-made grave, and by its side the bier was rested—while they paused a moment until holy words had been said. An idle boy, called there by curiosity, saw something lying on the fresh earth thrown out from the grave, which attracted his attention. A little blossom, the only one to be seen around, had grown exactly on the spot where the sexton chose to dig poor Kate's last resting place. It was a weak but lovely flower, and now lay where it had been carelessly thrown amid the coarse gravel. The boy twirled it a moment in his fingers—the bruised fragments gave out a momentary perfume, and then fell to the edge of the pit, over which the child at that moment leaned and gazed in his inquisitiveness. As they dropped they were wafted to the bottom of the grave. The last look was bestowed on the dead girl's face by those who loved her so well in life, and then she was softly laid away to that repose which, after life's fitful fever, comes so sweetly.

Yet in the churchyard on the hill is Dumb Kate's grave. There stands a little white stone at the head, and the grass grows richly there; and gossips, sometimes of a Sabbath afternoon, rambling over that gathering place of the gone from earth, stop awhile and con over the poor girl's hapless story.

———

THE LITTLE SLEIGHERS.
A SKETCH OF A WINTER MORNING ON THE BATTERY.

JUST before noon, one day last winter, when the pavements were crusted plentifully with ice-patches, and the sun, though shining out very brightly by fits and starts, seemed incapable of conveying any warmth, I took my thick overcoat, and prepared to sally forth on a walk. The wind whistled as I shut the door behind me, and when I turned the corner it made the most ferocious demonstrations toward my hat, which I was able to keep on my head not without considerable effort. My flesh quivered with the bitter coldness of the air. My breath appeared steam. Qu-foo-o! how the gust swept along!

Coming out into Broadway, I wended along by the Park, St. Paul's church, and the icicle-tipped trees in Trinity grave-yard. Having by this time warmed myself into a nice glow, I grew more comfortable, and felt ready to do any deed of daring that might present itself—even to the defiance of the elements which were growling so snappishly around me.

When I arrived at Battery-place—at the crossing which leads from that antique, two story, corner house, to the massive iron gates on the opposite side—I must confess that I was for a moment in doubt whether I had not better, after all, turn and retrace my steps. The wind absolutely roared. I could hear the piteous creaking of the trees on the Battery as the branches grated against one another, and could see how they were bent down by the power of the blast. Out in the bay the waves were rolling and rising, and over the thick rails which line the shore-walk dashed showers of spray, which fell upon the flag stones and froze there.

But it was a glorious and inspiring scene, with all its wildness. I gave an extra pull of my hat over my brows—a closer adjustment of my collar around my shoulders, and boldly ventured onward. I stepped over the crossing, and passed through the gate.

Ha! ha! Let the elements run riot! There is an exhilarating sensation—a most excellent and enviable fun—in steadily pushing forward against the stout winds!

The whole surface of the Battery was spread with snow. It seemed one mighty bride's couch, and was very brilliant, too, as though varnished with a clear and glassy wash. This huge, white sheet, glancing back a kind of impudent defiance to the sun, which shone sharply the while, was not, it seemed, to be left in its repose, or without an application to use and jollity. Many dozens of boys were there, with skates and small sleds—very busy. Oh, what a noisy and merry band!

The principal and choicest of the play tracks was in that avenue, the third from the water, known to summer idlers there as "Lovers' Walk."

For nearly its whole length it was a continued expanse of polished ice, made so partly by the evenness of the surface and partly by the labor of the boys. This fact I found out to my cost; for, turning in it before being aware that it was so fully preoccupied and so slippery, I found it necessary to use the utmost caution or run the certainty of a fall.

"Pawny-guttah!" Gentle lady, (I must here remark,) or worthy gentleman, as the case may be, whose countenance bends over this page, and whose opportunities have never led you to know the use, meaning and import, conveyed in the term just quoted—call to your side some bright-eyed boy—a brother or a son, or a neighbor's son, and ask him.

"Pawny-guttah!" I stepped aside instinctively, and, with the speed of an arrow there came gliding along, lying prone upon a sled, one of the boyish troop. The polished steel runners of his little vehicle sped over the ice with a slightly grating noise, and he directed his course by touching the toe of either boot, behind him, upon the ice, as he wished to swerve to the right or left.

Who can help loving a wild, thoughtless, heedless, joyous boy? Oh, let us do what we can—we who are past the time—let us do what we may to aid their pleasures and their little delights, and heal up their petty griefs. Wise is he who is himself a child at times. A man may keep his heart fresh and his nature youthful, by mixing much with that which is fresh and youthful. Why should we, in our riper years, despise these little people, and allow ourselves to think them of no higher consequence than trifles and unimportant toys?

I know not a prettier custom than that said to be prevalent in some parts of the world, of covering the corpses of children with flowers. They pass away, frail and blooming, and the blossom of a day is indeed their fittest emblem. Their greatest and worst crimes were but children's follies, and the sorrow which we indulge for their death has a delicate refinement about it, flowing from ideas of their innocence, their simple prattle, and their affectionate conduct while living. Try to love children. It is purer, and more like that of angels than any other love.

Reflections somewhat after this cast were passing in my mind as I paused a moment and gazed upon those little sleighers. What a miniature, too, were they of the chase of life! Everyone seemed intent upon his own puny objects—everyone in pursuit of "fun."

The days will come and go, and the seasons roll on, and these young creatures must grow up and launch out in the world. Who can foretell their destinies? Some will die early and be laid away in their brown beds of earth, and thus escape the thousand throes, and frivolities, and temptations, and miserable fictions and mockeries which are interwoven with our journey here on earth. Some will plod onward in the path of gain—that great idol of the world's worship—and have no higher aspirations than for profit upon merchandize. Some will love, and have those they love look coldly upon them; and then, in their sickness of heart, curse their own birth-hour. But all, all will repose at last.

   Why, what a sombre moralist I have become! Better were it to listen to the bell-like music of those children's voices; and, as I turn to wend my way homeward, imbue my fancy with a kindred glee and joyousness! Let me close these mottled reveries.

———

THE CHILD AND THE PROFLIGATE.

Look not upon the wine when it is red.

They say 'tis pleasant on the lip,
And merry on the brain—
They say it stirs the sluggish blood,
And dulls the tooth of pain.
Ay—but within its gloomy deeps
A stinging serpent, unseen, sleeps.

N. P. Willis

AMONG the victims of the passion for strong drink the greater part become so, I have observed, not from any ignorance of the danger of the path they pursue, but from weakness and irresolution of mind. To the abstemious it is almost impossible to convey an idea of the strength of the desire, formed, after a while, in a habitual drinker. No one can know, except him who has realized it himself. The world points with contempt at the inebriate, and laughs him to scorn that he does not turn from the error of his ways. But oh, if the gony of his struggles could be seen—if the vain and impotent efforts he makes to disentangle himself from the thralldom of his tyrant—if the sharp shame, the secret tears, the throes of mortification and conscious disgrace—were apparent to those who condemn so severely, one little drop of sorrow might certainly be mingled with their anger.

Now and then, though rarely, it does happen that something occurs which turns the tide and converts the drinker with the feelings I have mentioned into a reformed man. And it is strange to observe how small and trivial are frequently the causes of this change. A word merely, or an unimportant action, or a casual incident not out of the ordinary routine, forms the starting point whence the hitherto miserable one commences a reformation which ere long presents him to the world with a clearer head and a purer soul. Such a word, it may be—such an incident—stirs up the fountains of thought, brings back memories long passed away and awakens the man to beautiful and pathetic recollections of an earlier and more innocent age. Thus fully awakened, and with the genial influence of the time in all its sway over him, if the crisis turns for good, it will surely be consummated for good. But should it turn to wickedness again, God have mercy on the fated being!

The incidents of my little narrative are simple and unromantic enough, and yet I hope they will not be found without interest. I tell no tale of fiction either. There are those now in this metropolis who will peruse the tale and acknowledge in their own minds' consciousness of its unadorned truth.

Just after sunset, one evening in summer, that pleasant hour when the air is balmy, the light loses its glare and all around is imbued with soothing quiet, on the door step of a house there sat an elderly woman waiting the arrival of her son. The house was in a straggling village some fifty miles from New York city. She who sat on the door step was a widow; her neat white cap covered locks of gray, and her dress, though neat, was exceedingly homely. Her house—for the tenement she occupied was her own—was very little and very old. Trees clustered around it so thickly as almost to hide its color—that blackish gray color which belongs to old wooden houses that have never been painted; and to get in it you had to enter a little rickety gate and walk through a short path, bordered by carrot beds and beets and other vegetables. The son whom she was expecting was her only child. About a year before he had been bound apprentice to a rich farmer in the place, and after finishing his daily task he was in the habit of spending half an hour at his mother's. On the present occasion the shadows of night had settled heavily before the youth made his appearance. When he did, his walk was slow and dragging, and all his motions were languid, as if from great weariness. He opened the gate, came through the path and sat down by his mother in silence.

"You are sullen to-night, Charley," said the widow, after a moment's pause, when she found that he returned no answer to her greetings.

As she spoke she put her hand fondly on his head; it was as wet as if it had been dipped in the water. His shirt, too, was soaked; and as she passed her fingers down his shoulder she felt a sharp twinge in her heart, for she knew that moisture to be the heard-wrung sweat of severe toil, exacted from her young child (he was but thirteen years old) by an unyielding task master.

"You have worked hard to-day, my son."

"I've been mowing."

The widow's heart felt another pang.

"Not all day, Charley?" she said, in a low voice; and there was a slight quiver in it.

"Yes, mother, all day," replied the boy; "Mr. Ellis said he couldn't afford to hire men, for wages are so high. I've swung the scythe ever since an hour before sunrise. Feel of my hands."

There were blisters on them like great lumps. Tears started in the widow's eyes. She dared not trust herself with a reply, though her heart was bursting with the thought that she could not better his condition. There was no earthly means of support on which she had dependence enough to encourage her child in the wish she knew he was forming—the wish not uttered for the first time—to be freed from his bondage.

"Mother," at length said the boy, "I can stand it no longer. I cannot and will not stay at Mr. Ellis's. Ever since the day I first went into his house I've been a slave; and if I have to work there much longer I know I shall run away and go to sea or somewhere else. I'd as leave be in my grave as there." And the child burst into a passionate fit of weeping.

His mother was silent, for she was in deep grief herself. After some minutes had flown, however, she gathered sufficient self-possession to speak to her son in a soothing tone, endeavoring to win him from his sorrows and cheer up his heart. She told him that time was swift—that in the course of a few years he would be his own master—that all people have their troubles—with many other ready arguments which, though they had little effect in calming her own distress, she hoped would act as a solace to the disturbed temper of the boy. And as the half hour to which he was limited had now elapsed she took him by the hand and led him to the gate, to set forth on his return. The child seemed pacified, though occasionally one of those convulsive sighs that remain after a fit of weeping, would break from his throat. At the gate he threw his arms about his mother's neck; each pressed a long kiss on the lips of the other, and the youngster bent his steps toward his master's house.

As her child passed out of sight the widow returned, shut the gate and entered her lonesome room. There was no light in the old cottage that night—the heart of its occupant was dark and cheerless. Love, agony, and grief, and tears, and convulsive wrestlings were there. The thought of a beloved son condemned to labor—labor that would break down a man—struggling from day to day under the hard rule of a soulless gold-worshipper; the knowledge that years must pass thus; the sickening idea of her own poverty and of living mainly on the grudged charity of neighbors—thoughts, too, of former happy days—these racked the widow's heart and made her bed a sleepless one and without repose.

The boy bent his steps to his employer's, as has been said. In his way down the village street he had to pass a public house, the only one the place contained; and when he came off against it he heard the sound of a fiddle—drowned, however, at intervals, by much laughter and talking. The windows were up, and the house standing close to the road, Charles thought it no harm to take a look and see what was going on within. Half a dozen footsteps brought him to the low casement, on which he leaned his elbow and where he had a full view of the room and its occupants. In one corner was an old man, known in the village as Black Dave—he it was whose musical performances had a moment before drawn Charles's attention to the tavern; and he it was who now exerted himself in a violent manner to give, with divers flourishes and extra twangs, a tune popular among that thick lipped race whose fondness for melody is so well known. In the middle of the room were five or six sailors, some of them quite drunk and others in the earlier stages of that process, while on benches around were more sailors and here and there a person dressed in landsmen's attire, but hardly behind the sea gentlemen in uproar and mirth. The individuals in the middle of the room were dancing; that is, they were going through certain contortions and shufflings, varied occasionally by exceedingly hearty stamps upon the sanded floor. In short, the whole party were engaged in a drunken frolic, which was in no respect different from a thousand other drunken frolics, except, perhaps, that there was less than the ordinary amount of anger and quarrelling. Indeed everyone seemed in remarkably good humor.

But what excited the boy's attention more than any other object was an individual, seated on one of the benches opposite, who, though evidently enjoying the spree as much as if he were an old hand at such business, seemed in every other particular to be far out of his element. His appearance was youthful. He might have been twenty-one or two years old. His countenance was intelligent and had the air of city life and society. He was dressed, not gaudily, but in every respect fashionably; his coat being of the finest black broadcloth, his linen delicate and spotless as snow, and his whole aspect that of one whose counterpart may now and then be seen upon the pave in Broadway of a fine afternoon. He laughed and talked with the rest, and it must be confessed his jokes—like the most of those that passed current there—were by no means distinguished for their refinement or purity. Near the door was a small table, covered with decanters and with glasses, some of which had been used, but were used again indiscriminately, and a box of very thick and very long cigars.

One of the sailors—and it was he who made the largest share of the hubbub—had but one eye. His chin and cheeks were covered with large bushy whiskers, and altogether he had quite a brutal appearance.

"Come, boys," said this gentleman; "come, let us take a drink! I know you're all a getting dry. So, curse me if you sha'n't have a suck at my expense."

This polite invitation was responded to by a general moving of the company toward the table holding the before mentioned decanters and glasses. Clustering there around, each one helped himself to a very handsome portion of that particular liquor which suited his fancy; and steadiness and accuracy being at that moment by no means distinguishing traits of the arms and legs of the party, a goodly amount of the fluid was spilled upon the floor. This piece of extravagance excited the ire of the personage who gave the "treat;" and that ire was still farther increased when he discovered two or three loiterers who seemed disposed to slight his request to drink. Charles, as we have before mentioned, was looking in at the window.

"Walk up, boys! walk up! Don't let there be any skulker among us, or blast my eyes if he shan't go down on his marrow bones and taste the liquor we have spilt! Hallo!" he exclaimed as he spied Charles; "hallo, you chap in the window, come here and take a sup!"

As he spoke he stepped to the open casement, put his brawny hands under the boy's arms and lifted him into the room bodily.

"There, my lads," said he, turning to his companions, "There's a new recruit for you. Not so coarse a one, either," he added as he took a fair view of the boy, who, though not what is called pretty, was fresh and manly looking, and large for his age.

"Come, youngster, take a glass," he continued. And he poured one nearly full of strong brandy.

Now Charles was not exactly frightened, for he was a lively fellow, and had often been at the country merry-makings and at the parties of the place; but he was certainly rather abashed at his abrupt introduction to the midst of strangers. So, putting the glass aside, he looked up with a pleasant smile in his new acquaintance's face.

"I've no need of anything now," he said, "but I'm just as much obliged to you as if I was."

"Poh! man, drink it down," rejoined the sailor; "drink it down—it won't hurt you."

And, by way of showing its excellence, the one-eyed worthy drained it himself to the last drop. Then filling it again, he renewed his efforts to make the lad go through the same operation.

"I've no occasion. Besides, my mother has often prayed me not to drink, and I promised to obey her."

A little irritated by his continued refusals, the sailor, with a loud oath, declared that Charles should swallow the brandy, whether he would or no. Placing one of his tremendous paws on the back of the boy's head, with the other he thrust the edge of the glass to his lips, swearing, at the same time, that if he shook it so as to spill its contents the consequences would be of a nature by no means agreeable to his back and shoulders.

Disliking the liquor, and angry at the attempt to overbear him, the undaunted child lifted his hand and struck the arm of the sailor with a blow so sudden that the glass fell and was smashed to pieces on the floor; while the liquid was about equally divided between the face of Charles, the clothes of the sailor, and the sand. By this time the whole of the company had their attention drawn to the scene. Some of them laughed when they saw Charles's undisguised antipathy to the drink; but they laughed still more heartily when he discomfited the sailor. All of them, however, were content to let the matter go as chance would have it—all but the young man of the black coat, who has before been spoken of.

What was there in the words which Charles had spoken that carried the mind of the young man back to former times—to a period when he was more pure and innocent than now? "My mother has often prayed me not to drink!" Ah, how the mist of months rolled aside and presented to his soul's eye the picture of his mother, and the sound of an injunction conveyed in almost those very words! Why was it, too, that the young man's heart moved with a feeling of kindness toward the harshly treated child? Was it that his assocations had hitherto been among the vile, and the contrast was now so strikingly great? Even in the hurried walks of life and business may we meet with beings who seem to touch the fountains of our love, and draw forth their swelling waters! The wish to love and be beloved, which the forms of custom and the engrossing anxiety for gain so generally smother, will sometimes burst forth in spite of all obstacles; and kindled by one who, till the hour, was unknown to us, will burn with a permanent and pure brightness!

Charles stood, his cheek flushed and his heart throbbing, wiping the trickling drops from his face with a handkerchief. At first the sailor, between his drunkenness and his surprise, was much in the condition of one suddenly awakened out of a deep sleep, who cannot call his consciousness about him. When he saw the state of things, however, and heard the jeering laugh of his companions, his dull eye, lighting up with anger, fell upon the boy who had withstood him. He seized Charles with a grip of iron, and with the side of his heavy boot gave him a sharp and solid kick. He was about repeating the performance—for the child hung like a rag in his grasp—but all of a sudden his ears rang, as if pistols were snapped close to them; lights of various hues flickered in his eye, (he had but one, it will be remembered,) and a strong propelling power caused him to move from his position, and keep moving until he was brought up by the wall. A blow, a cuff given in such scientific and effectual manner that the hand from which it proceeded was evidently no stranger to the pugilistic art, had been suddenly planted in the ear of the sailor. It was planted by the young man of the black coat. He had watched with interest the proceedings of the sailor and the boy—two or three times he was on the point of interfering, and when the kick was given, his rage was uncontrollable. He sprang from his seat, and assuming, unconsciously however, the attitude of a boxer, he struck the sailor in a manner to cause those unpleasant sensations which have been described. And he would probably have followed up the attack in a manner by no means consistent with the sailor's personal safety, had not Charles, now thoroughly terrified, clung round his legs and prevented his advancing.

The scene was a strange one, and for the time quite a silent one. The company had started from their seats, and for a moment held breathless but strained positions. In the middle of the room stood the young man, in his not at all ungraceful attitude—every nerve out, and his eyes flashing brilliantly. He seemed rooted like a rock; and clasping him, with an appearance of confidence in his protection, hung the boy.

"Dare! you scoundrel!" cried the young man, his voice thick with passion, "dare to touch this boy again, and I'll thrash you till no sense is left in your body."

The sailor, now partially recovered, made some gestures of a belligerent nature.

"Come on, drunken brute!" continued the angry youth; "I wish you would! You've not had half what you deserve!"

Upon sobriety and sense more fully taking their place in the brains of the one-eyed mariner, however, that worthy determined in his own mind that it would be most prudent to let the matter drop. Expressing therefore his conviction to that effect, adding certain remarks to the purport that he "meant no harm to the lad," that he was surprised at such a gentleman being angry at "a little piece of fun," and so forth—he proposed that the company should go on with their jollity just as if nothing had happened. In truth, he of the single eye was not a bad fellow at heart, after all; the fiery enemy whose advances he had so often courted that night, had stolen away his good feelings and set busy devils at work within him, that might have made his hands do some dreadful deed had not the stranger interposed.

In a few minutes the frolic of the party was upon its former footing. The young man sat down upon one of the benches, with the boy by his side, and while the rest were loudly laughing and talking they two conversed together. The stranger learned from Charles all the particulars of his simple story—how his father had died years since—how his mother worked hard for a bare living—and how he himself, for many dreary months, had been the servant of a hard hearted, avaricious master. More and more interested, drawing the child close to his side, the young man listened to his plainly told history—and thus an hour passed away.

It was now past midnight. The young man told Charles that on the morrow he would take steps to relieve him from his servitude—that for the present night the landlord would probably give him a lodging at the inn—and little persuading did the host need for that.

As he retired to sleep very pleasant thoughts filled the mind of the young man—thoughts of a worthy action performed—thoughts, too, newly awakened ones, of walking in a steadier and wiser path than formerly.

That roof, then, sheltered two beings that night—one of them innocent and sinless of all wrong—the other—oh, to that other what evil had not been present, either in action or to his desires!

Who was the stranger? To those that, from ties of relationship or otherwise, felt an interest in him, the answer to that question was not pleasant to dwell upon. His name was Langton—parentless—a dissipated young man—a brawler—one whose too frequent companions were rowdies, blacklegs and swindlers. The New York police officers were not strangers to his countenance; and certain reporters, who notice the proceedings there, had more than once received a fee for leaving out his name from the disgraceful notoriety of their columns. He had been bred to the profession of medicine; besides, he had a very respectable income, and his house was in a pleasant street on the west side of the city. Little of his time, however, did Mr. John Langton spend at his domestic hearth; and the elderly lady who officiated as his housekeeper was by no means surprised to have him gone for a week or a month at a time, and she knowing nothing of his whereabouts.

Living as did, the young man was an unhappy being. It was not so much that his associates were below his own capacity—for Langton, though sensible and well bred, was by no means talented or refined—but that he lived without any steady purpose, that he had no one to attract him to his home, that he too easily allowed himself to be tempted—which caused his life to be, of late, one continued scene of dissatisfaction. This dissatisfaction he sought to drive away (ah, foolish youth!) by the brandy bottle, and mixing in all kinds of parties where the object was pleasure. On the present occasion he had left the city a few days before, and was passing his time at a place near the village where Charles and his mother lived. He fell in, during the day, with those who were his companions of the tavern spree; and thus it happened that they were all together. Langton hesitated not to make himself at home with any associate that suited his fancy.

The next morning the poor widow rose from her sleepless cot; and from that lucky trait in our nature which makes one extreme follow another, she set about her toil with a lightened heart. Ellis, the farmer, rose, too, short as the nights were, an hour before day; for his god was gain, and a prime article of his creed was to get as much work as possible from everyone around him. He roused up all his people, and finding that Charles had not been home the preceding night, he muttered threats against him, and calling a messenger, to whom he hinted that any minutes which he stayed beyond an exceeding short period would be subtracted from his breakfast time, dispatched him to the widow's to find what was her son about.

He roused up all his people, and finding that Charles had not been home the preceding night, he muttered threats against him, and calling a messenger, to whom he hinted that any minutes which he stayed beyond a most exceeding short period, would be subtracted from his breakfast time, dispatched him to the widow's to find what was her son about.

What was he about? He had a beautiful dream—and thus it was in seeming.

With one of the brightest and earliest rays of the warm sun a gentle angel entered his apartment, and hovered over him, and looked down with a pleasant smile, and blessed him. And the child thought his benefactor, the young man, was nigh, sleeping also. Noiselessly taking a stand by the bed, the angel bent over the boy's face and whispered strange words into his ear; it seemed to him like soft and delicate music. So the angel, pausing a moment, and smiling another and a doubly sweet smile, and drinking in the scene with his large soft eyes, bent over again to the boy's lips and touched them with a kiss, as the languid wind touches a flower. He seemed to be going now, and yet he lingered. Twice or thrice he bent over the brow of the young man—and went not. Now the angel was troubled; for he would have pressed the young man's lips with a kiss, as he did the child's—but a spirit from Heaven, who touches anything tainted by evil thoughts, does it at the risk of having his breast pierced with pain, as with a barbed arrow. At that moment a very pale, bright ray of sunlight darted through the window and settled on the young man's features. Then the beautiful spirit knew that permission was granted him; so he softly touched the young man's face with his, and silently and swiftly wafted himself away on the unseen air.

In the course of the day Ellis was called upon by young Langton, and never perhaps in his life was the farmer puzzled more than at the young man's proposals—his desire to provide for the widow's family, a family that could do him no pecuniary good, and his willingness to disburse money for that purpose. In that department of Ellis's structure where the mind was, or ought to have been situated, there never had entered the slightest thought assimilating to those which actuated the young man in his benevolent movements. Yet Ellis was a church member and a county officer.

The widow, too, was called upon, not only on that day, but the next and the next.

It needs not that I should particularize the subsequent events of Langton's and the boy's history—how the reformation of the profligate might be dated to begin from that time—how he gradually severed the guilty ties that had so long galled him—how he enjoyed his own home again—how the friendship of Charles and himself grew not slack with time—and how, when in the course of seasons he became head of a family of his own, he would shudder at the remembrance of his early dangers and his escapes. Often, in the bustle of day and the silence of night, would he bless the utterance of those words, "My mother prayed me not to drink!"

Loved reader, own you the moral interwoven in this simple story? Let your children read it. To them draw forth the moral—pause a moment ere your eye wander to a different page—and dwell upon it.

SHIRVAL: A TALE OF JERUSALEM.

EARTH, this huge clod over which we tread, enwraps the lost outlines, the mixed remains, of myriads of human forms that were once as we are now. Nor is the truth a stale one, old as it may be. Also, it is a beautiful and solemn truth.

Those buried men and women lived and loved—wrought and grieved, like us;—had their crimes and their agonies, as the living now have. Death came to their dwellings and struck down those for whom affection was strong. Anger and hate and pride, three wicked ministers of unhappiness, held sway over them;—love and charity, too, stole into their hearts, and found a home there. And thus they were, and thus they passed away.—O Earth! huge tomb-yard of humanity! if the brown pall under which are hidden the things of old ages—of ancient generations—of the men who have been folded in thy recesses when thyself wast in the earlier life—if that far-stretching pall could be removed, what eye might look unquailed on the awful wonders of the scene!

Let me go to times and people away in the twilight of years past. It is the pen's prerogative to roll back the curtains of centuries that can have a real existence no more, and make them live in fiction—pleasing thus, and, haply, fostering thoughts which the moralist would smile upon. Such are among the sweetest rewards of us humble bookmen, whose spur comes in the hope that we may gain, not alone for our frail paragraphs, some passing thought of friendliness to ourselves, from a portion of that outer world we love so well.

Very beauteous was the coming of the sun, one day, over the cities of JUDAH. The tops of the mountains, which received his first warm kisses, smiled down upon each neighboring valley; and the Israelites and dark-eyed women went forth to their tasks with cheerful hearts. The dewy grass, and the olive trees, glittered as with countless diamonds. All nature was glad like a laughing infant.

But in a street in a city of NAIN stood the house of tears—the house of the widow UNNI, whose son, the preceding night, had been forsaken, by the angels of Life, and now lay a cold corpse in the inner chamber. And there came a young Jewish maid, early in the morning, and went into the chamber. Her cheeks, as she walked through the fresh air, were like the roses of the plains of SHARON; but when she passed the portals, and entered, and saw the dead man, her face imaged the colour of ashes, the emblem of mourning and decay. The maid was ZAR, the beloved of SHIRVAL, the widow's son. Her mission was to inquire about his illness: she found it ended.

Noon came.—The preparations for the burial had been made, and ere the daylight should close, the body of the youth was to be put in its sepulchre, without the walls of the town.

He looked beautiful in his manly proportions, even in death. The curls of his hair were drawn back from his forehead, and a linen bandage had been passed under his chin, and tied around his face. And on one side stood his mother, and on the other side ZAR, his beloved. UNNI wept, and rent the air with shrieks of agony; but the maid was silent and tearless.

Twenty-and-four years had SHIRVAL lived in his native city; and it was known that his mother, to whom he was ever obedient, leaned on him as the staff of her declining age. He was her only child.

"O, God of Judgments!" cried UNNI, "what am I that thou hast afflicted me thus!"

And her grey hairs were bowed to the ground, and she would not receive consolation.

So as the young man's body lay there, the day still waned, and the mourners arrived to attend him to the last resting-place. They placed the corpse upon the bier, and set forth.

No one could tell why it was so,—that, as they advanced, many spectators, people of NAIN, gathered around them, and walked with them on their solemn errand. The rich men and the officers joined the crowd; and it swelled to many hundreds. Yet none spoke, or understood what mysterious impulse led him thus to honour the funeral-march of the poor widow's son.

Now they came to the gates of the town, and the foremost mourners passed out, and went no farther; for a band of travelers were before them, coming inward, and stopped the way. The travelers paused too—all but a small group who approached the mourners of SHIRVAL. Most of those in the group were wayworn and coarse in their appearance; but their look imported strange things—and ONE of their number as HE walked a little before the rest, fixed all eyes, while the hearts of the wide assembly throbbed, as at the nearness of an UNDEFINABLE PRESENCE, more than mortal.

The BEING was of middle stature and fair proportions, in every motion whereof was easy grace. His step was neither rapid or very slow; and his look more sought the earth than swept around him with glances of pride. His face was beautifully clear, and his eyes, blue as the sky above them, beamed forth benevolence and love. His brown hair was parted in the middle of his head, and flowed in heavy ringlets down upon his shoulders. The aspect of the stranger was not deficient in dignity, but it seemed far unlike the dignity of princes and captains.

As this PRESENCE came in among them, the haughtiest of NAIN were awed: and the concourse paused, with the expectation, as it were, of an unwonted event. It needed not that anyone should inform the BEING what had happened. SHIRVAL's corpse was there, borne upon its bier; and the widow was nigh, convulsed in her grief; and ZAR, the maiden, followed meekly.

A moment only were the compassionate eyes of the BEING bent upon this sight of agony and death—bent with a mortal look of sympathy. He stept forth, and stood before UNNI. He spoke,—and his voice, musical and manly, thrilled to the fine chords of every soul in that multitude.

"Widow of NAIN," he said, "weep not!"

And he looked about, and waived his hand gently; and as he touched the bier with one finger, they who carried it put it upon the ground, and stood away. And the stranger bent over the young man's corpse, and gazed upon the face.

O, Nazarine! thou who didst pour out bloody sweat upon the cross, at the Place of Skulls! what feelings of human pity—what yearning for the weal of all mankind—what prophetic horror at the agonies of thine own death—what sympathy with the woes of earth, which the mortality of thy nature gave thee to feel as mortals themselves feel—what soul-tears for that pain and wretchedness, which must still continue through time—what of all these were thine during that fearful minute, it were almost blasphemous to transcribe!

There was a stillness over all the gathering. Even the grief of UNNI was hushed. The people had given back from around the BEING, and he and the dead form were together—all eyes bent toward them.

A second time he spoke—and at the awful nature of the command he gave, the hearts of the people paused in motion, and the breathings were suspended.

"Live! thou who art dead!—Arise, and speak to the woman, thy mother!"

At the word, the white vestments wherewith they had bound SHIRVAL began to move. His eyes unclosed, and the colour came back into his cheeks. The lips that had been still, parted a passage for the misty breath,—and the leaden fingers glowed with the warmth of life. The ashy hue of his skin was marked by the creeping blood, as it started to fulfil its circulation in the veins—and the nostrils quivered at the inward and outward motion of air. His limbs felt the wondrous impulse—he rose, and stood up among them, wrapped in his shroud and the white linen.

"I have slept!" said he, turning to his mother, "but there have been no dreams."

And he kissed the widow's cheek, and smiled pleasantly on ZAR. Then the awe of the presence of the Stranger gathered like a mantle upon him—and the three knelt upon the ground and bent their faces on the earth-worn sandals of the MAN OF WO.

———

RICHARD PARKER'S WIDOW.

WHEN I was in London some years since, I, with another person, went one morning to the police office, with several of the higher functionaries with whom my companion was acquainted. After seeing some of the peculiar sights and scenes that are to be met with at such a place only, we were invited to sit a while in a sort of half-private, half-public parlour, attached to the establishment. When we entered, one of the magistrates was talking to an aged, shabbily-dressed lady, (for lady she was, by a title superior to dress,) who seemed to be applying for parish assistance, or making enquiries of him about the necessary steps to be taken for procuring it. My companion, the moment he saw her, directed my attention to her by a peculiar movement of the head.

"Look closely at her," said he, in a whisper, "that woman's life has been indirectly involved with the welfare of nations. When we are alone, I will tell you more about her."

The female might at one time have been handsome; but now, years and sorrow had graven deeply on her features and form the evidences of decay. Her eyes had that piercing look which belongs to people whose sight is nearly gone. Her garments were clean, though old, and very faded.

I was interested in the appearance of this female—though I could hardly divine what or who she had been—and when we left the place, I reminded my friend of his promise.

"That woman," said he, "is the widow of a man whose name, forty years ago, rang for many weeks like a death-knell through ENGLAND, and shook with terror the foundation of the throne itself! Her husband was RICHARD PARKER, the Admiral Mutineer, who headed the sailor's rebellion at the NORE."

He then went on to give me the particulars of this celebrated mutiny, which I had read in my own country when a boy, but which had nearly escaped my memory. As the reader may also have forgotten—or may never have heard it—and as the history of the singular affair is full of interest—I will recapitulate it here. I am of course indebted to English authorities for most of the facts that follow.

In the early part of MAY, 1797, the British seamen in the vessels about the NORE, (a point of land so called, dividing the mouths of the THAMES and MEDWAY,) indignant at many oppressive restrictions, and at non-payment of their wages, broke out into an organized meeting. They deprived the officers of all command of the ships, though they otherwise treated them with every respect. Each vessel was put under the government of a committee of twelve men; and a board of delegates was appointed to represent the whole body of sailors, each man-of-war sending two delegates, and each gun-boat one. Of these delegates RICHARD PARKER was chosen president. This man was of good family, and had been engaged in SCOTLAND in mercantile business, which proving unsuccessful, he one day in a fit of despondency left his family, took the bounty, and became a common sailor. He was gentlemanly in his manners, well educated, and the bravest of the brave.

The force of the mutineers, which, toward the latter part of MAY, consisted of twenty-four sail, soon proceeded to block up the THAMES—sternly refusing a passage to vessels up or down. In a day or two there was of course an immense number of ships, and water craft of all descriptions, under detention. The appearance of the whole fleet is described by contemporaneous accounts as appalling and grand. The red flag floated from the mast-head of every one of the mutineers.

It may well be imagined that the alarm of the citizens of LONDON was extreme. The government, however, though unable to quell PARKER and his fellow sailors by force, remained firm in their demand of unconditional surrender as a necessary preliminary to any intercourse. This, perhaps, was the wisest line of conduct they could have assumed. The seamen never seemed to think of taking an offensive attitude. Being thus left in quiet to meditate on their position of hostility to a whole country, they shortly began to grow timorous—and the more so, as the government had caused all the buoys to be removed from the mouth of the THAMES and the adjacent coasts, so that no vessel dare attempt to move away, for fear of running aground. The mutineers held together, nevertheless, till the 30th of MAY, when the Clyde frigate was carried off through a combination of its officers with some of the seamen; and this desertion was followed by the ST. FIORENZO. Both were fired upon by the mutineers, but no great damage was done.

From the 1st to the 10th of JUNE, all was disquiet on board the fleet. Several more desertions happened during that period. On the 10th, the whole body of the detained merchantmen were allowed, by common consent, to proceed up the river. Such a multitude of ships certainly never entered a port before at one tide. On the 12th, only seven ships held out—and by the 16th, the mutiny had terminated. A party of soldiers then went on board the SANDWICH, and to them were surrendered the delegates of that ship, RICHARD PARKER, and a man named DAVIES. PARKER, to whom the title of Admiral was given by the sailors and the public during the whole of this affair, occupied from the beginning the principal attention of the government. He was now brought summarily to trial before a naval court martial, on the 22d of JUNE—having been thrown, for the intermediate time, in the black hole of SHEERNESS garrison. In his defence, which he conducted himself, he read an elegantly written and powerful paper, setting forth that the situation he had held, had been in a measure forced upon him—that he had consented to occupy it chiefly for the purpose of preventing any bloody or cruel measures—that he had restrained the men from excesses—and that, had he been disloyal, he might have taken the ship to sea, or to an enemy's port.

But nothing could save PARKER. He was sentenced to death. When his doom was pronounced, he immediately stood up, and with a firm voice made the following short but most beautiful response: "I shall submit to your sentence with all due respect, being confident of the innocence of my intentions, and that GOD will receive me into favor: and I sincerely hope that my death will be the means of restoring tranquility to the navy, and that those men who have been implicated in the business may be reinstated in their former situations, and again be serviceable to their country."

On the morning of the 30th JUNE, the whole fleet was ranged a little below SHEERNESS, in full sight of the SANDWICH, on board of which RICHARD PARKER was that day to suffer an ignominious death. The yellow flag, the signal of death, was hoisted—and the crew of every ship was piped to the forecastle. PARKER was aroused from a sound sleep that morning, and attired himself with neatness, in a suit of deep mourning. He mentioned to his attendants that he had made a will, leaving his wife heir to some property belonging to him. On coming upon deck, he was hale, but perfectly composed, and drank a glass of water4 "to the salvation of his soul, and the forgiveness of all his enemies." He said nothing to his mates on the forecastle but "Good bye to you!" and expressed a hope that his death would be considered a sufficient atonement, and would save the lives of others. He was then strung up at the yard arm, and in a few moments dangled lifeless there.

Mrs. PARKER was in SCOTLAND, among her connexions, and when the rumour came to her ears that the NORE fleet had mutinied, and that the leader was one RICHARD PARKER, she immediately started for London—and on her arrival heard that her husband had been tried, but the result was unknown. Being able to think of nothing better than petitioning the king, she gave a person a guinea to draw up a paper, praying that PARKER'S life might be spared. She attempted to make her way with this to His Majesty's presence—but was finally obliged to hand it to a Lord in waiting, who gave her the cruel intelligence that applications for mercy in all cases would be attended to, except those for RICHARD PARKER. The distracted woman then took coach for ROCHESTER on the 29th, where she got on board a king's ship, and learned that her husband was to be executed on the following day. Who can imagine her unspeakable wretchedness, as she sat up the whole of that long night of agony! At four o'clock the next morning, she went to the river side to hire a boat to take her to the SANDWICH, that she might at least bid her poor husband farewell. Her feelings had been deeply tortured by hearing every person she met talking of that occurrence which was the subject of her distress; and now the first waterman to whom she spoke, answered, "No, I cannot take one passenger; the brave Admiral PARKER is to be hung to-day, and I will get any sum I choose to ask for a party!"

After a long trial, the wretched wife was glad to get on board a SHEERNESS market-boat—but no boat was allowed to come alongside the SANDWICH. In her desperation, she called on PARKER by name, and prevailed on the boat people, by the mere spectacle of her suffering, to attempt to go nearer, when they were stopped by a sentinel threatening to fire at them. As the hour drew nigh, she saw her husband appear on deck between two clergymen. She called on him again, and he heard her voice, for he exclaimed, "There is my dear wife, from SCOTLAND!"

The excitement of this was too great, and the miserable wife fell back in a state of insensibility—from which she was fortunate enough not to recover until the scene of death was finished, and she had been taken ashore. She seemed to think, however, that she was yet in time; she hired another boat, and a second time reached the SANDWICH. Her delirious shriek, "Pass the word for RICHARD PARKER!" rang through the decks, and must have startled all on board. The truth was now made clear to her, and she was further informed that the body had just been taken on shore for burial. She immediately caused herself to be rowed back again, and proceeded to the churchyard; but found the ceremony over and the gate locked!

The key, which she sought from the proper source, was refused her; and she was excited almost to madness at learning that the surgeon would probably disinter the body that night for anatomical purposes. She was now in a situation of mind wherein all the ordinary timidity and softness of her sex left her. She waited cautiously around the churchyard 'til dusk—then, clambering over the wall, she readily found her husband's new-made grave. The shell was not buried deep, and she worked in such a manner that the earth was soon scraped away, and the coffin lid removed. She clasped the cold neck, and kissed the clammy lips of the object of her search!

The necessity of prompt measures to possess the body, aroused this extraordinary woman from the enjoyment of her melancholy pleasure. She left the churchyard, and communicated her situation to two women, who in their turn got several men to undertake the task of lifting the body. This was accomplished successfully, and the coffin was carried to ROCHESTER, and thence to LONDON. The widow stopped with her sad burthen at a tavern on TOWER HILL. By express at the same hour, or before it, information had been brought to the capital of the exhumation of the body; and the secret of its locality could not now be kept. A great crowd assembled around the house, anxious to see the dead man's face, which Mrs. PARKER would not permit. She had the corpse in her own room, and was sitting disconsolately beside it, hardly knowing what course to pursue, and fearing it would be taken from her by the authorities, when the Lord Mayor arrived to see her. He came to ask what she intended doing with the remains of her husband: she answered, "to inter them decently at EXETER, or in SCOTLAND." The Lord Mayor said the body should not be taken from her; but he prevailed upon her to have it buried in LONDON. Arrangements were accordingly made for that purpose, and finally the corpse of the hapless sailor was inhumed in Whitechapel churchyard. After the closing ceremony, Mrs. PARKER gave a certificate that the burial had been conducted to her satisfaction. But, though strictly questioned as to who had aided her in the disinterment, she firmly refused to disclose their names.

  For many years afterward, this faithful wife lived on the income she derived from the little property left her by her husband's will. But ultimately her rights were somehow or other decided against by a judicial tribunal, and she was thrown into great poverty in LONDON, where she lived. She was in the habit of receiving assistance, however, from the highest quarters. WILLIAM IV gave her at one time £20, and at another £10. On the occasion when I saw her in 1836, she was nearly blind, and, as I intimated in the beginning, was making application for some public aid. I was gratified to learn afterward that she received it. Whether she be yet living, I am not able to say.

———

THE BOY-LOVER.

LISTEN, and the old will speak a chronicle for the ears of the young! It is a brave thing to call up the memory of fires long burnt out—at least we withered folk believe so—and delight so to act.

Ah, youth! thou art one day coming to be old, too! And let me tell thee how thou mayest get a useful lesson. For an hour, dream thyself old. Realize, in thy thoughts and consciousness, that vigor and strength are subdued in thy sinews—that the color of the shroud is likened in thy very hairs—that all those leaping desires, luxurious hopes, beautiful aspirations, and proud confidences, of thy younger life, have long been buried, (a funeral for the better part of thee) in that grave which must soon close over thy tottering limbs. Look back, then, over the long track of the past years. How has it been with thee? Are there bright beacons of happiness enjoyed, and of good done by the way? Glimmer gentle rays of what was scattered from a holy heart? Have benevolence, and love, and undeviating honesty left tokens on which thy eyes can rest sweetly? Is it well with thee, thus? Answerest thou, It is? Or answerest thou, I see nothing but gloom and shattered hours, and the wreck of good resolves, and a broken heart, filled with sickness, and troubled among its ruined chambers, with the phantoms of many follies?

O, youth! youth! this dream will one day be a reality—a reality, either of heavenly peace, or agonizing sorrow.

And yet not for all is it decreed to attain the neighborhood of the three-score and ten years—the span of human life.

I am to speak of one who died young. Very awkward was his childhood!—but most fragile and sensitive! So delicate a nature may exist in a rough, unnoticed plant! Let the boy rest;—he was not beautiful, and drooped away betimes. But for the cause—it is a singular story, to which let crusted worldlings pay the tribute of a light laugh—light and empty as their own hollow hearts.

The sway of love over the mind—though the old subject of flippant remarks from those who are too coarse to appreciate its delicate ascendency—is a strange and beautiful thing. And in your dream of age, young man, which I have charged you to dream, sad and desolate will that trodden path appear, over which have not been shed the rose tints of this Light of Life.

Love! the mighty passion which, ever since the world began, has been conquering the great, and subduing the humble—bending princes, and mighty warriors, and the famous men of all nations, to the ground before it. Love! the delirious hope of youth, and the fond memory of old age. Love! which, with its cankerseed of decay within, has sent young men and maidens to a longed-for, but too premature burial. Love! the child-monarch that Death itself cannot conquer; that has its tokens on slabs at the head of grass-covered tombs—tokens more visible to the eye of the stranger, yet not so deeply graven as the face and the remembrances cut upon the heart of the living. Love! the sweet, the pure, the innocent; yet the cause of fierce hate, of wishes for deadly revenge, of bloody deeds, and madness, and the horrors of hell. Love! that wanders over battlefields, turning up mangled human trunks, and parting back the hair from gory faces, and daring the points of swords and the thunder of artillery, without a fear or a thought of danger.

Words! words! I begin to see I am, indeed, an old man, and garrulous! Let me go back—yes, I see it must be many years!

It was at the close of the last century. I was at that time studying law, the profession my father followed. One of his clients, was a widow, an elderly Swiss woman, who kept a little ale-house, on the banks of the North River, at about two miles from what is now the centre of the city. Then, the spot was quite out of town, and surrounded by fields and green trees. The widow often invited me to come and pay her a visit, when I had a leisure afternoon—including also in the invitation, my brother, and two other students who were in my father's office. Matthew, the brother I mention, was a boy of sixteen; he was troubled with an inward illness—though it had no power over his temper, which ever retained the most admirable placidity and gentleness. He was cheerful, but never boisterous, and everybody loved him; his mind seemed more developed than is usual for his age, though his personal appearance was exceedingly plain. Wheaton and Brown, the names of the other students, were spirited, clever young fellows, with most of the traits that those in their position of life generally possess. The first was as generous and brave as any man I ever knew. He was very passionate, too, but the whirlwind soon blew over, and left everything quiet again. Frank Brown was slim, graceful and handsome. He professed to be fond of sentiment, and used to fall regularly in love once a month.

The half of every Wednesday we four youths had to ourselves, and were in the habit of taking a sail, a ride, or a walk together. One of these afternoons, of a pleasant day in April, the sun shining and the air clear, I bethought myself of the widow and her beer—about which latter article I had made inquiries, and heard it spoken of in terms of high commendation. I mentioned the matter to Matthew and to my fellow-students, and we agreed to fill up our holiday by a jaunt to the ale-house. Accordingly, we set forth, and, after a fine walk, arrived in glorious spirits, at our destination.

Ah! how shall I describe the quiet beauties of the spot, with its long low piazza looking out upon the river, and its clean homely tables, and the tankards of real silver in which the ale was given us, and the flavor of that excellent liquor itself. There was the widow; and there was a sober, stately old woman, half companion, half servant, Margery by name; and there was (good God! my fingers quiver yet as I write the word!) young Ninon, the daughter of the widow.

O, through the years that live no more, my memory strays back, and that whole scene comes up before me once again—and the brightest part of the picture is the strange ethereal beauty of that young girl! She was apparently about the age of my brother Matthew, and the most fascinating, artless creature I had ever beheld. She had blue eyes, and light hair, and an expression of childish simplicity, which was charming to behold. I have no doubt that ere half an hour had elapsed from the time we entered the tavern, and saw Ninon, every one of the four of us loved the girl to the very depth of passion.

We neither spent so much money, nor drank as much beer, as we had intended before starting from home. The widow was very civil, being pleased to see us, and Margery served our wants with a deal of politeness—but it was to Ninon that the afternoon's pleasure was attributable; for though we were strangers, we became acquainted at once—the manners of the girl, merry as she was, putting entirely out of view the most distant imputation of indecorum—and the presence of the widow and Margery, (for we were all in the common room together, there being no other company,) serving to make us all disembarassed and at ease.

It was not until quite a while after sunset, that we started on our return to the city. We made several attempts to revive the mirth and lively talk that usually signalized our rambles, but they seemed forced and discordant, like laughter in a sick room. My brother was the only one who preserved his usual tenor of temper and conduct.

I need hardly say that thenceforward every Wednesday afternoon was spent at the widow's tavern. Strangely, neither Matthew, or my two friends, or myself, spoke to each other, of the sentiment that filled us, in reference to Ninon. Yet we all knew the thoughts and feelings of the others; and each, perhaps, felt confident that his love alone was unsuspected by his companions.

The story of the widow was a touching yet simple one. She was by birth a Swiss. In one of the cantons of her native land, she had grown up, and married, and lived for a time in happy comfort. A son was born to her, and a daughter, the beautiful Ninon. By some reverse of fortune, the father and head of the family had the greater portion of his possessions swept from him. He struggled for a time against the evil influence, but it pressed upon him harder and harder. He had heard of a people in the western world—a new and swarming land—where the stranger was welcomed, and peace and the protection of the strong arm thrown around him. He had not heart to stay and struggle amid the scenes of his former prosperity, and he determined to go and make his home in that distant republic of the west. So with his wife and children, and the proceeds of what little property was left, he took passage for New York. He was never to reach his journey's end. Either the cares that weighed upon his mind, or some other cause consigned him to a sick hammock, from which he only found relief through the Great Dismisser. He was buried in the sea; and in due time, his family arrived at the American emporium. But there, the son, too, sickened—died, ere long, and was buried likewise. They would not bury him in the city, but away—by the solitary banks of the Hudson; on which the widow soon afterwards took up her abode, nearby him.

Ninon was too young to feel much grief at these sad occurrences; and the mother, whatever she might have suffered inwardly, had a good deal of phelgm and patience, and set about making herself and her remaining child as comfortable as might be. They had still a respectable sum in cash, and after due deliberation, the widow purchased the little quiet tavern, not far from the grave of her boy; and of Sundays and holidays she took in considerable money—enough to make a decent support for them in their humble way of living. French and Germans visited the house frequently, and quite a number of young Americans too. Probably the greatest attraction to the latter was the sweet face of Ninon.

Spring passed, and summer crept in and wasted away, and autumn had arrived. Every New Yorker knows what delicious weather we have, in these regions, of the early October days; how calm, clear, and divested of sultriness, is the air, and how decently Nature seems preparing for her winter sleep.

Thus it was of the last Wednesday we started on our accustomed excursion.—Six months had elapsed since our first visit, and, as then, we were full of the exuberance of young and joyful hearts. Frequent and hearty were our jokes, by no means particular about the theme or the method, and long and loud the peals of laughter that rang over the fields, or along the shore.

We took our seats round the same clean, white table, and received our favorite beverage in the same bright tankards. They were set before us by the sober Margery, no one else being visible. As frequently happened, we were the only company. Walking, and breathing the keen fine air, had made us dry, and we soon drained the foaming vessels, and called for more. I remember well an animated chat we had about some poems that had just made their appearance from a great British author, and were creating quite a public stir. There was one, a tale of passion and despair, which Wheaton had read, and of which he gave us a transcript. It seemed a wild, startling, dreamy thing, and perhaps it threw over our minds its peculiar cast.

An hour moved off, and we began to think it strange that neither Ninon or the widow came into the room. One of us gave a hint to that effect to Margery; but she made no answer, and went on in her usual way as before.

"The grim old thing," said Wheaton, "if she were in Spain, they'd make her a premier duenna!"

I asked the woman about Ninon and the widow. She seemed disturbed, I thought; but making no reply to the first part of my question, said that her mistress was in another part of the house, and did not wish to be with company.

"Then be kind enough, Mrs. Vinegar," resumed Wheaton good-naturedly, "be kind enough to go and ask the widow if we can see Ninon."

Our attendant's face turned as pale as ashes, and she precipitately left the apartment. We laughed at her agitation, which Frank Brown assigned to our merry ridicule.

Quite a quarter of an hour elapsed before Margery's return. When she appeared, she told us briefly that the widow had bidden her obey our behest, and now, if we desired, she would conduct us to the daughter's presence. There was a singular expression in the woman's eyes, and the whole affair began to strike us as somewhat odd; but we arose, and taking our caps, followed her as she stepped through the door.

Back of the house were some fields, and a path leading into clumps of trees. At some thirty rods distant from the tavern, nigh one of those clumps, the larger tree whereof was a willow, Margery stopped, and pausing a minute, while we came up, spoke in tones calm and low:

"Ninon is there!"

She pointed downward with her finger. Great God! There was a grave, new-made, and with the sods loosely joined, and a rough brown stone at each extremity! Some earth yet lay upon the grass near by—and amid the whole scene our eyes took in nothing but that horrible covering of death—the oven-shaped mound! My sight seemed to waver, my head felt dizzy, and a feeling of deadly sickness came over me. I heard a stifled exclamation, and looking round saw Frank Brown leaning against the nearest tree, great sweat upon his forehead, and his cheeks bloodless as chalk.

Wheaton gave way to his agony more fully than ever I had known a man before; he had fallen down upon the grass—sobbing like a child, and wringing his hands. It is impossible to describe that spectacle—the suddenness and fearfulness of the sickening truth that came upon us like a stroke of thunder!

Of all of us, my brother Matthew neither shed tears, or turned pale, or fainted, or exposed any other evidence of inward depth of pain. His quiet pleasant voice was indeed a tone lower, but it was that which recalled us, after the lapse of many long minutes, to ourselves.

So the girl had died and been buried. We were told of an illness that had seized her the very day after our last preceding visit; but we inquired not into the particulars.

And now come I to the conclusion of my story, and to the most singular part of it. The evening of the third day afterward, Wheaton, who had wept scalding tears, and Brown, whose cheeks had recovered their color, and myself, that for an hour thought my heart would never rebound again from the fearful shock—that evening, I say, we three were seated around a table in another tavern, drinking other beer, and laughing but a little less cheerfully, and as though we had never known the widow or her daughter—neither of whom, I venture to affirm, came into our minds once the whole night, or but to be dismissed again, carelessly, like the remembrance of faces seen in a crowd.

Strange are the contradictions of the things of life! The seventh day after that dreadful visit saw my brother Matthew—the delicate one, who, while bold men writhed in torture, had kept the same placid face, and the same untrembling fingers—him that seventh day saw a clay-cold corpse, shrouded in white linen, and carried to the repose of the churchyard. The shaft, rankling far down and within, wrought a poison too great for show, and the youth died.

———

THE DEATH OF WIND-FOOT.

THREE hundred years ago—so heard I the tale, not long since, from the mouth of one educated like a white man, but born of the race of whom Logan and Tecumseh sprang,—three hundred years ago, there lived on lands now forming an eastern county of the most powerful of the American states, a petty Indian tribe governed by a brave and wise chieftain. This chieftain was called by a name which in our language signifies Unrelenting. His deeds of courage and subtlety made him renowned through no small portion of the northern continent. There were only two dwellers in his lodge—himself and his youthful son; for twenty moons had filled and waned since his wife, following four of her offspring, was placed in the burial ground.

As the Unrelenting sat alone one evening in his rude hut, one of his people came to inform him that a traveler from a distant tribe had entered the village, and desired food and repose. Such a petition was never slighted by the red man; and the messenger was sent back with an invitation for the stranger to abide in the lodge of the chief himself. Among that simple race, no duties were considered more honorable than arranging the household comforts of a guest: those duties were now performed by the host's own hand, his son having not yet returned from the hunt on which he had started with a few young companions at early dawn. In a little while the wayfarer was led into the dwelling by him who had given the first notice of his arrival.

"You are welcome, my brother," said the Unrelenting.

The person to whom this kind salute was addressed was an athletic Indian, apparently of middle age, and habited in the scant attire of his species. He had the war-tuft on his forehead, under which flashed a pair of brilliant eyes. His rejoinder was friendly and brief.

"The chief's tent is lonesome—his people are away?" continued the stranger, after a pause, casting a glance of inquiry around.

"My brother says true that it is lonesome," the other answered. "Twelve seasons ago, the Unrelenting saw five children in the shadow of his wigwam, and their mother was dear to him. He was strong, like a cord of many fibres. Then the breath of Manito snapped the fibres one by one asunder. He looked with a pleasant eye on my sons and daughters, and wished them for himself. Behold all that is left to brighten my heart!"

The Unrelenting turned as he spoke, and pointed to an object just inside the opening of the tent.

A moment or two before, the figure of a boy had glided noiselessly in, and taken his station back of the chief. Hardly twelve years seemed the age of the new-comer. He was a noble child! His limbs, never distorted with the ligatures of civilized life, were as graceful as the ash, and symmetrical and springy as the bounding stag's. It was the last and loveliest of the chieftain's sons—the soft-lipped, nimble Wind-Foot.

With the youth's assistance, the preparations for their frugal meal were soon completed. After finishing it, as the stranger appeared to be weary, a heap of skins was arranged for him in one corner of the lodge, and he laid himself down to sleep.

It was a lovely summer evening. The moon shone, the stars twinkled, and the thousand voices of a forest night sounded in every direction. The chief and his son reclined at the opening of the tent, enjoying the cool breeze which blew freshly upon them, and flapped the piece of deer-hide that served for their door, sometimes flinging it down so as to darken the apartment, then raising it suddenly up again, as if to let in the bright moonbeams.

Wind-Foot spoke of his hunt that day. He had met with no success, and, in a boy's impatient spirit, wondered why it was that others' arrows should hit the mark, and failure be reserved for him alone. The chief heard him with a sad smile, as he remembered his own youthful traits; he soothed the child with gentle words, telling him that brave warriors sometimes went whole days with the same perverse fortune.

"Many years since," said the chief, "when my cheek was soft, and my arms felt the numbness of but few winters, I myself vainly traversed our hunting grounds, as you have done to-day. The Dark Influence was around me, and not a single shaft would do my bidding."

"And my father brought home nothing to his lodge?" asked the boy.

"The Unrelenting came back without any game," the other answered; "but he brought what was dearer to him and his people than the fattest deer or the sweetest bird-meat—he brought the scalp of an accursed Kansi!"

The voice of the chief was deep and sharp in its tone of hatred.

"Will my father," said Wind-Foot, "tell—"

The child started, and paused. An exclamation, a sudden guttural noise, came from that part of the tent where the stranger was sleeping. The dry skins which formed the bed rustled, as if he who lay there was changing his position, and then all continued silent. The Unrelenting proceeded in a lower tone, fearful that they had almost broken the slumber of their guest.

"Listen!" said he: "you know a part, but not all the cause of hatred there is between our nation and the abhorred enemies whose name I mentioned.—Longer back than I can remember, they did mortal wrong to your fathers. The scalps of two of your near kindred hang in Kansi lodges, and I have sworn, my son, to bear them a never-ending hatred.

"On the morning of which I spoke, I started with fresh limbs and a light heart to search for game. Hour after hour, I roamed the forest with no success; and at the setting of the sun, I found myself weary, and many miles from my father's lodge. I laid down at the foot of a tree, and sleep came over me. In the depth of the night, a voice seemed whispering in my ears; it called me to rise quickly—to look around. I started to my feet, and found no one there but myself: then I knew that the Dream-Spirit had been with me. As I cast my eyes about in the gloom, I saw a distant brightness. Treading softly, I approached. The light was that of a fire, and by the fire lay two sleeping figures. O, I laughed the quiet laugh of a deathly mind, as I saw who they were—a Kansi warrior, and a child, like you, my son, in age. I felt the edge of my tomahawk—it was keen as my hate. I crept toward them as the snake crawls through the grass. I bent over the slumbering boy; I raised my weapon to strike. But I thought that were they both slain no one would carry the tale to the Kansi tribe. My vengeance would be tasteless to me if they knew it not—and I spared the child. Then I glided to the other; his face was of the same cast as the first, which gladdened me, for then I knew they were of close kindred. I raised my arm—I gathered my strength—I struck, and cleft the warrior's brain in quivering halves!"

The chief had gradually wrought himself up to a pitch of loudness and rage, and his hoarse tones at the last part of his narration, rang croakingly through the lodge.

At that moment, the deer-hide curtain kept all within in darkness; the next, it was lifted up, and a flood of the moonlight filled the apartment. A startling sight was back there, then! The strange Indian was sitting up on his couch, his distorted features glaring toward the unconscious ones in front, with a look like that of Satan to his antagonist angel.

His lips were parted, his teeth clenched, his arm raised, and his hand doubled—every nerve and sinew in bold relief. This spectacle of fear lasted only for a moment; the Indian at once sank noiselessly back, and lay with the skins wrapped round him as before.

It was now an advanced hour of the night. Wind-Foot felt exhausted by his day's travel; the father and son arose from their seat at the door, and retired to rest. In a little while, all was silence in the tent; but from the darkness which surrounded the bed of the stranger, flashed two fiery orbs, rolling about incessantly like the eyes of an angry wild beast. The lids of those orbs closed not in slumber during the night.

Among the former inhabitants of this continent, it was considered rudeness, of the highest degree, to annoy a traveler or a guest with questions about himself, his last abode or his future destination. Until he saw fit to go, he was made welcome to stay, whether for a short time or a long one. Thus, on the morrow, when the strange Indian showed no signs of departing, the chief expressed not the least surprise, but felt indeed a compliment indirectly paid to his powers of entertainment.

Early the succeeding day, the Unrelenting called his son to him, while the stranger was standing at the tent-door. He told Wind-Foot that he was going on a short journey, to perform which and return, would probably take him till night-fall. He enjoined the boy to remit no duties of hospitality toward his guest, and bade him be ready at evening with a welcome for his father.

The sun had marked the middle of the afternoon—when the chief, finishing what he had to do sooner than he expected, came back to his own dwelling, and threw himself on the floor to obtain rest,—for the day though pleasant, had been a warm one. Wind-Foot was not there, and after a little interval the chief stepped to a lodge nearby to make inquiry after him.

"The young brave," said a woman, who appeared to answer his questions, "went away with the chief's strange guest many hours since."

The Unrelenting turned to go back to his tent.

"I cannot tell the meaning of it," added the woman, "but he of the fiery eye, bade me, should the father of Wind-Foot ask about him, say to the chief these words, 'Unless your foe sees you drink his blood, that blood loses more than half its sweetness!'"

The Unrelenting started as if a scorpion had stung him. His lip trembled, and his hand involuntarily moved to the handle of his tomahawk. Did his ears perform their office truly? Those sounds were not new to him. Like a floating mist, the gloom of past years rolled away in his memory, and he recollected that the words the woman spake were the very ones he himself had uttered to the Kansi child whose father he slew long, long ago, in the forest! And this stranger? Ah, now he saw it all. He remembered the dark looks of his guest—and carrying his mind back again, traced the features of the Kansi in their matured counterpart. And the chief felt too conscious for what terrible purpose Wind-Foot was in the hands of this man. He sallied forth, gathered together a few of his warriors, and started swiftly to seek his child.

About the same hour that the Unrelenting returned from his journey, Wind-Foot, several miles from home, was just coming up to his companion, who had gone on a few rods ahead of him, and was at that moment seated on the body of a fallen tree, a mighty giant of the woods that some whirlwind had tumbled to the earth. The child had roamed about with his new acquaintance through one path and another with the heedlessness of his age; and now while the latter sat in perfect silence for several minutes, Wind-Foot idly sported near him. It was a solemn spot; in every direction around were towering patriarchs of the wilderness, growing and decaying in solitude.

At length the stranger spoke: "Wind-Foot!"

The child, who was but a few yards off, approached at the call. As he came near, he stopped in alarm; his companion's eyes had that dreadfully bright glitter again—and while they looked at each other, terrible forebodings arose in the boy's soul.

"Young chieftan," said the stranger, "you must die!"

"The brave is in play," was the response, "Wind-Foot is a little boy."

"Serpents are small at first," replied the savage, "but in a few moons they have fangs and deadly poison. Hearken, branch from an evil root!—I am a Kansi!—The youth your parent spared in the forest has now become a man. Warriors of his tribe point to him and say, 'His father's scalp adorns the lodge of the Unrelenting, but the wgiwam of the Kansi is bare!'—Wind-Foot! it must be bare no longer!"

The boy's heart beat quickly—but beat true to the stern courage of his ancestors.

"I am the son of a chief," he answered, "my cheeks cannot be wet with tears."

The Kansi looked at him a few seconds with admiration, which soon gave way to malignant scowls. Then producing from an inner part of his dress a withe of some tough bark, he stepped to Wind-Foot, and began binding his hands. It was useless to attempt resistance, for besides the disparity of their strength, the boy was unarmed, while the savage had at his waist a hatchet, and a rude stone weapon resembling a poniard. He pointed to Wind-Foot the direction he must take, gave a significant touch at his girdle, and followed close on behind.

When the Unrelenting and his people started to seek for the child and that fearful stranger, they were lucky enough to find the trail which the absent ones had made. None except an Indian's eye could have tracked them by so slight and devious a guide. But the chief's sight was sharp with paternal love: they followed on—winding, and on again—at length coming to the fallen tree. The train was now less irregular, and they traversed it with greater rapidity. Its direction seemed towards the shores of a long narrow lake which lay adjacent to their territory. Onward went they, and as the sun sank in the west, they saw his last flitting gleams reflected from the waters of the lake. The grounds here were almost clear of trees; and as they came out, the Unrelenting and his warriors swept the range with their keen eyes.

Was it so indeed?—There, on the grass not twenty rods from the shore, were the persons they sought—and fastened nearby was a canoe. They saw from his posture that the captive was bound; they saw, too, that if the Kansi should once get him in the boat, and gain a start for the opposite side, where very likely some of his tribe were waiting for him, release would be almost impossible. For a moment only they paused. Then the Unrelenting sprang off, uttering the battle cry of his tribe, and the rest joined in the terrible chorus and followed him.

As the sudden sound was swept along by the breeze to the Kansi's ear, he jumped to his feet, and with that wonderful self-possession which distinguishes his species, determined at once what was safest and surest for him to do. He seized Wind-Foot by the shoulder, and ran toward the boat, holding the boy's person as a shield from any weapons the pursuers might attempt to launch after him. He possessed still the advantage. It was a fearful race; and the Unrelenting felt his heart grow sick, as the Indian, dragging his child, approached nearer to the water's edge.

"Turn, whelp of a Kansi!" the chief madly cried. "Turn, thou whose coward arm warrest against children! Turn, if thou darest, and meet the eye of a full-grown brave!"

A loud taunting laugh was borne back from his flying enemy to the ears of the furious father. The savage did not look around, but twisted his left arm, and pointed with his finger to Wind-Foot's throat. At that moment, he was within twice his length of the canoe. The boy heard his father's voice, and gathered his energies, faint and bruised as he was, for a last struggle. Vain his efforts! for a moment only he loosened himself from the grip of his foe, and fell upon the ground. That moment, however, was a fatal one to the Kansi. With the speed of lightning, the chief's bow was up at his shoulder—the cord twanged sharply—and a poison-tipped arrow sped through the air. Faithful to its mission, it cleft the Indian's side, just as he was stooping to lift Wind-Foot in the boat. He gave a wild shriek; his blood spouted from the wound, and he staggered down upon the sand. His strength, however, was not yet gone. Hate and measureless revenge—the stronger that they were baffled—raged within him, and shot through his eyes, glassy as they were beginning to be with death-damps. Twisting his body like a bruised snake, he worked himself close up to the bandaged Wind-Foot. He felt to his waistband, and drew forth the weapon of stone. He laughed a laugh of horrid triumph—he shouted aloud—and just as the death-rattle sounded in his throat, the instrument (the shuddering eyes of the child saw it, and shut their lids in intense agony,) came down, driven too surely to the heart of the hapless boy.

When the Unrelenting came up to his son, the last signs of life were fading in the boy's countenance. His eyes opened and turned to the chief; his beautiful lips parted in a smile, the last effort of expiring fondness. On his features flitted a lovely look, transient as the ripple athwart the wave, a slight tremor shook him, and the next minute Wind-Foot was dead.

———

REVENGE AND REQUITAL.
A TALE OF A MURDERER ESCAPED

I.

THAT section of Nassau-street which runs into the great mart of New York brokers and stock-jobbing, has for a long time been much occupied by practitioners of the law. Tolerably well known amid this class some years since, was Adam Covert, a middle aged man of rather limited means, who, to tell the truth, gained more by trickery than he did in the legitimate and honorable exercise of his profession. He was a tall, bilious-faced widower; the father of two children; and had lately been seeking to better his fortunes by a rich marriage. But somehow or other his wooing did not seem to thrive well, and, with perhaps one exception, the lawyer's prospects in the matrimonial way were hopelessly gloomy.

Among the early clients of Mr. Covert, had been a distant relative, named Marsh, who, dying somewhat suddenly, left his son and daughter, and some little property to the care of Covert, under a will drawn up by that gentleman himself. At no time caught without his eyes open, the cunning lawyer, aided by much sad confusion in the emergency which had caused his services to be called for, and disguising his object under a cloud of technicalities, inserted provisions in the will giving himself an almost arbitrary control over the property and over those for whom it was designed. This control was even made to extend beyond the time when the children would arrive at mature age. The son, Philip, a spirited and high-tempered fellow, had some time since passed that age. Esther, the girl, a plain and somewhat devotional young woman, was in her nineteenth year.

Having such power over his wards, Covert did not scruple openly to use his advantage, in pressing his claims as a suitor for Esther's hand. Since the death of Marsh, the property he left, which had been in real estate, and was to be divided equally between the brother and sister, had risen to very considerable value; and Esther's share was, to a man in Covert's situation, a prize very well worth seeking. In all this time, while really owning a respectable income, the young orphans often felt the want of the smallest sums of money, and Esther, on Philip's account, was more than once driven to various contrivances—the pawn-shop, sales of her own little luxuries, and the like, to furnish him with means.

Though she had frequently shown her guardian unequivocal evidence of her aversion, Esther continued to suffer from his persecutions, until one day he proceeded farther and was more pressing than usual. She possessed some of her brother's mettlesome temper, and gave him an abrupt and most decided refusal. With dignity she exposed the baseness of his conduct, and forbade him ever again mentioning marriage to her. He retorted bitterly, vaunted his hold on her and Philip, and swore an oath that unless she became his wife, they should both thenceforward be penniless. Losing his habitual self-control in his exasperation, he even added insults such as women never receives from any one deserving the name of man, and at his own convenience left the house. That day, Philip returned to New York, after an absence of several weeks on the business of a mercantile house in whose employment he had lately engaged.

Toward the latter part of the same afternoon, Mr. Covert was sitting in his office, in Nassau-street, busily at work, when a knock at the door announced a visitor, and directly afterward young Marsh entered the room. His face exhibited a peculiar pallid appearance that did not strike Covert at all agreeably, and he called his clerk from an adjoining room, and gave him something to do at a desk nearby.

"I wish to see you alone, Mr. Covert, if convenient," said the new comer.

"We can talk quite well enough where we are," answered the lawyer: "indeed, I don't know that I have any leisure to talk at all, for just now I am very much pressed with business."

"But I must speak to you," rejoined Philip sternly, "at least I must say one thing, and that is, Mr. Covert, that you are a villain!"

"Insolent!" exclaimed the lawyer, rising behind the table and pointing to the door; "Do you see that, sir? Let one minute longer find you the other side of it, or your feet may reach the landing by a quicker method than usual. Begone, sir!"

Such a threat was the more harsh to Philip, for he had rather high-strung feelings of honor. He grew almost livid with suppressed agony.

"I will see you again very soon," said he, in a low but distinct manner, his lips trembling as he spoke; and he turned at once and left the office.

The incidents of the rest of that pleasant summer day left little impression on the young man's mind. He roamed to and fro without any object or destination. Along South-street, and by Whitehall, he watched with curious eyes the movements of the shipping, and the loading and unloading of cargoes; and listened to the merry heave-yo of the sailors and stevedores. There are some minds upon which great excitement produces the singular effect of uniting two utterly inconsistent faculties—a sort of cold apathy, and a sharp sensitiveness to all that is going on at the same time. Philip's was one of this sort; he noticed the various differences in the apparel of a gang of wharf-laborers; turned over in his brain whether they received wages enough to keep them comfortable, and their families also—and if they had families or not, which he tried to tell by their looks. In such petty reflections the daylight passed away. And all the while the master wish of Philip's thoughts was a desire to see the lawyer Covert. For what purpose he himself was by no means clear.

II.

Nightfall came at last. Still, however, the young man did not direct his steps homeward. He felt more calm, however, and entering an eating-house ordered something for his supper, which, when it was brought to him, he merely tasted and strolled forth again. There was a kind of gnawing sensation of thirst within him yet, and as he passed a hotel, he bethought him that one little glass of spirits would, perhaps, be just the thing. He drank, and hour after hour wore away unconsciously; he drank not one glass, but three or four, and strong glasses they were to him, for he was habitually abstemious.

It had been a hot day and evening, and when Philip, at an advanced period of the night emerged from the bar-room into the street, he found that a thunderstorm had just commenced. He resolutely walked on, however, although at every step it grew more and more blustering.

The rain now poured down a cataract; the shops were all shut; few of the street lamps were lighted; and there was little except the frequent flashes of lightning to show him his way. When along about half the length of Chatham-street, which lay in the direction he had to take, the momentary fury of the tempest, forced him to turn aside into a sort of shelter formed by the corners of the deep entrance to a Jew pawnbroker's shop there. He had hardly drawn himself in as closely as possible when the lightning revealed to him that the opposite corner of the nook was tenanted also.

"A sharp rain this," said the other occupant, who simultaneously beheld Philip.

The voice sounded to the young man's ears a note which almost made him sober again. It was certainly the voice of Adam Covert. He made some commonplace reply, and waited for a flash of lightning to show him the stranger's face. It came, and he saw that his companion was, indeed, his guardian.

Philip Marsh had drank deeply—(let us plead all that may be possible to you, stern moralist). Upon his mind came swarming, and he could not drive them away, thoughts of all those insults his sister had told him of, and the bitter words Covert had spoken to her; he reflected, too, on the injuries Esther as well as himself had received, and were still likely to receive, at the hands of that bold, bad man—how mean, selfish, and unprincipled was his character—what base and cruel advantages he had taken of many poor people, entangled in his power, and of how much wrong and suffering he had been the author, and might be again through future years. The very turmoil of the elements, the harsh roll of the thunder, the vindictive beating of the rain, and the fierce glare of the wild fluid that seemed to riot in the ferocity of the storm around him, kindled a strange sympathetic fury in the young man's mind. Heaven itself (so deranged were his imaginings) appeared to have provided a fitting scene and time for a deed of retribution, which to his disordered passion half wore the semblance of a divine justice. He remembered not the ready solution to be found in Covert's pressure of business which had no doubt kept him later than usual; but fancied some mysterious intent in the ordaining that he should be there, and that they two should meet at that untimely hour. All this whirl of influence came over Philip with startling quickness at that horrid moment. He stepped to the side of his guardian.

"Ho!" said he, "have we met so soon, Mr. Covert? You traitor to my dead father—robber of his children!—scoundrel!—wretch! I fear to think on what I think now!"

The lawyer's natural effrontery did not desert him.

"Unless you'd like to spend a night in the watch-house, young gentleman," said he, after a short pause, "move on. Your father was a weak man, I remember; as for his son, his own wicked heart is his worst foe. I have never done wrong to either—that I can say, and swear it!"

"Insolent liar!" exclaimed Philip, his eyes flashing out sparks of fire in the darkness.

Covert made no reply except a cool, contemptuous laugh.

This stung the excited young man to double fury. He sprang upon the lawyer, and clutched him by the neckcloth.

"Take it then!" he cried hoarsely, for his throat was impeded by the fiendish rage which in that black hour possessed the wretched young man. "You are not fit to live!"

He dragged his guardian to the earth, and fell crushingly upon him, choking the shriek the poor victim but just began to utter. Then, with monstrous imprecations, he twisted a tight knot around the gasping creature's neck, drew a clasp-knife from his pocket, and touching the spring, the long sharp blade, too eager for its bloody work, flew open.

During the lull of the storm, the last strength of the prostrate man burst forth into one short loud cry of agony. At the same instant the arm of the murderer thrust the blade once, twice, thrice deep in his enemy's bosom! Not a minute had passed since that fatal, exasperating laugh.—but the deed was done, and the instinctive thought which came at once to the guilty one, was a thought of fear and escape.

In the unearthly pause which followed, Philip's eyes gave one long searching sweep in every direction, above and around him. Above! God of the all-seeing eye! What, and who was that white figure there?

"Forbear! In Jehovah's name forbear!" cried a shrill but clear and melodious voice.

It was as if some accusing spirit had come down to bear witness against the deed of blood. Leaning far out of an upper window, appeared a white-draperied shape, its face possessed of a wonderful youthful beauty. Long vivid glows of lightning gave Philip a full opportunity to see as clearly as though the sun had been shining at noon-day. One hand of the figure was raised upward in a deprecating attitude, and his large bright black eyes bent down upon the scene below with an expression of horror and shrinking pain. Such heavenly looks, and the peculiar circumstances of the time, filled Philip's heart with awe.

"O, if it is not yet too late," spoke the youth again, "spare him! In God's voice I command, 'Thou shalt do no murder!'"

The words rang like a knell in the ear of the terror-stricken and already remorseful Philip. Springing from the body, he gave a second glance up and down the walk, which was totally lonesome and deserted; then crossing into Reade street, he made his fearful way in a state half of stupor, half bewilderment, by the nearest avenues to his home.

III.

When the corpse of the murdered lawyer was found in the morning, and the officers of justice commenced their inquiry, suspicion immediately fell upon Philip, and he was arrested. The most rigorous search, however, brought to light nothing at all implicating the young man, except his visit to Covert's office the evening before, and his angry language there. That was by no means enough to fix so heavy a charge upon him.

The second day afterward, the whole business came before the ordinary judicial tribunal, in order that Philip might be either committed for the crime or discharged. The testimony of Mr. Covert's clerk stood alone. One of his employers, who, believing in his innocence, had deserted him not in this crisis, had provided him with the ablest criminal counsel in New York. The proof was declared entirely insufficient, and Philip was discharged.

The crowded court-room made way for him as he came out; hundreds of curious looks fixed upon his features, and many a jibe passed upon him. But of all that arena of human faces, he saw only one—a sad, pale, black-eyed one, cowering in the centre of the rest. He had seen that face twice before—the first time as a warning spectre—the second time in prison, immediately after his arrest—now for the last time! This young stranger—this son of a scorned and persecuted race—coming to the court-room to perform an unhappy duty, with the intention of testifying to what he had seen, melted at the sight of Philip's bloodless cheek, and of his sister's convulsive throbs, and forbore witnessing against the murderer. Shall we applaud or condemn him? Let every reader answer the question for himself.

That afternoon Philip left New York. His friendly employer owned a small farm some miles up the Hudson, and until the excitement of the affair was over, he advised the young man to go thither. Philip thankfully accepted the proposal, made a few preparations, took a hurried leave of Esther, with a sad foreboding, which indeed proved true, that he should see her no more on earth, and by nightfall was settled in his new abode.

And how, think you, rested Philip Marsh that night? Rested indeed! O, if those who clamor so much for the halter and the scaffold to punish crime, could have seen that sight, they might have learned a lesson then! Four days had elapsed since he that lay tossing upon the bed there, had slumbered. Not the slightest intermission had come to his awakened and tensely strung sense, during those frightful days. And now, O, pitying Heaven, if he could only lose his remorse in one little hour of wholesome respose!

Disturbed waking dreams came to him, as he thought what he might do to gain his lost peace. Far, far away would he go! The cold roll of the murdered man's eye, as it turned up its last glance into his face—the shrill exclamation of pain—all the unearthly vividness of the posture, motions, and looks of the dead—the warning voice from above—pursued him like tormenting furies, and were never absent from his mind, asleep or awake, that long weary night! Anything, any place, to escape such horrid companionship! He would travel inland—hire himself to do hard drudgery upon some farm—work incessantly through the wide summer days, and thus force nature to bestow oblivion upon his senses, at least a little while now and then. He would fly on, on, on, until, amid different scenes and a new life, the old memories were rubbed entirely out. He would fight bravely in himself for peace of mind. For peace he would labor and struggle—for peace he would pray!

At length, after a feverish slumber of some thirty or forty minutes, the unhappy youth, waking with a nervous start, raised himself in bed, and saw the blessed day-light beginning to dawn. He felt the sweat trickling down his naked breast; the sheet where he had lain was quite wet with it. Dragging himself wearily, he opened the window.

Ah! that good morning air—how it refreshed him—how he leaned out, and drank in the fragrance of the blossoms below, and almost for the first time in his life felt how beautifully indeed God had made the earth, and that there was wonderful sweetness in mere existence! And amidst the thousand mute mouths eloquent eyes, which appeared as it were to look up and speak in every direction, he almost fancied so many invitations to come forth, and be among them. Not without effort, for he was very weak, he dressed himself, and issued forth into the open air.

Clouds of pale gold and transparent crimson draperied the eastern sky, but the sun, whose face gladdened them into all that glory, was not yet above the horizon. It was a time and place of such rare, such Eden-like beauty! Philip paused at the summit of an upward slope, and gazed around him. Some few miles off, he could see a gleam of the Hudson river—and above it, a spur of those rugged cliffs that are scattered along its western shores. Nearer by were cultivated fields. The clover grew richly there, the young grain bent to the early breeze, and the air was filled with an intoxicating perfume from the neighboring apple-orchards, snowy in their luxuriant bloom. At his side was the large well-kept garden of his host, in which were many pretty flowers, grass-plots, and a wide avenue of noble trees. As Philip gazed, the holy calming power of Nature—the invisible spirit of so much beauty, and so much innocence, melted into his soul. The disturbed passions and the feverish conflict subsided. He even felt something like that envied peace of mind—a sort of joy even in the presence of all the unmarred goodness. It was as fair to him, guilty though he had been, as to the purest of the pure. No accusing frowns saw he in the face of the flowers, or in the green shrubs, and the branches of the trees. They, more forgiving than mankind, and distinguishing not between the children of darkness and the children of light—they at least treated him with gentleness. Was he, then, a being so accursed? Involuntarily, he bent over a branch of red roses, and took them softly between his hands, those murderous bloody hands! But the red roses neither withered nor smelled less fragrant. And as the young man kissed them, and dropped a tear upon them, it seemed to him that he had found pity and sympathy from heaven itself.

IV.

After desolating the cities of the eastern world, the dreaded Cholera made its appearance on our American shores. In New York, hardly had the first few cases occurred, when thousands of the inhabitants precipitately left town, and sought safety in the neighboring country districts. For various reasons, however, large numbers still remained. While fear drove away so many—poverty, quite as stern a force, also compelled many to stay where they were. The desire of gain, too, made a large number continue their business as usual, for composition was narrowed down, and profits were large. Besides these, there was, of the number who remained, still another class, every name among whom is brightly kept in the records writ by God's angels. These were the men and women, heedless of their own small comfort, who went out amid the diseased, the destitute, and the dying, like merciful spirits—wiping the drops from hot brows, and soothing the agony of cramped limbs—speaking words of consolation to many a despairing creature, who would else have been vanquished by his soul's weakness alone—and treading softly but quickly from bedside to bedside, with those little offices which are so grateful to the sick, but which can so seldom be obtained from strangers. O, Charity and Love! sister throbbings in the heart of great Humanity! Sweetly, but ever surely, step you forth from the very tempest of those horrors, which whirl away by wholesale man's virtue and his life! Even in carnage and pestilence, sad fruits of the evil that will work from ourselves—when hate, selfishness, and all monstrous vice threaten to beat the good utterly out of mortal hearts—the Genius of Perfection which our Maker gave us, springs up loftily and cheerfully from the ruin, and laughs to scorn the taunts of those malignant fiends, who please themselves in the depression of our better nature! Yes: then, to cancel the weight of wickedness, appear large deeds of devotion and love;—then come forth heroes of charity and brotherly kindness, whose meek courage is greater than the courage of war;—then favorite messengers of heaven enter into the hearts of noble women, who go forth and relieve the scene of its sombre gloom, like lamps at night. And though the number be few, their sum of holiness affords a leaven large enough for the freshness and healthiness of an otherwise unwholesome world! Ye true sons and daughters of Christ! I bow before you with a reverence I never pay either to earthly rank or intellectual majesty!

Such, during the cholera season in New York, was the character of a small and sacred band who, with no union except the union of that sublimest of impulses, good will to man, went wherever they could find themselves needed or useful. One among them seemed even more ardent and devoted than the rest. Wherever the worst cases of the contagion were to be found, he also was to be found. In noisome alleys and foul rear-buildings, in damp cellars and hot garrets, thither came he with food, medicine, gentle words, and gentle smiles. By the head of the dying, the sight of his pale calm face and his eyes moist with tears of sympathy, often divested death of its severest terrors. At midnight hovered he over the forms of sick children, hushing their fretful cries, solacing them to rest with a soft voice, and cooling their hot cheeks with his own hands and lips, disdainful of the peril he inhaled at every breath. At night, too, when not occupied with other cares, he went prying and peering about, threading that dirtiest and wretchedest section of the city, between Chatham and Centre streets, pausing frequently, and gazing hither and thither. And when his well trained ear caught those familiar sounds, those wailings of anguish and fear, how unerringly would he direct his feet to the spot whence they proceeded. There, like an unearthly help, vouchsafed from above, he would at once take the measures experience had proved most efficacious, not seldom finding his reward the next day in the recovered safety of his patient.

This messenger of health to many, and peace to all, this unwearied, unterrified angel of mercy and charity, was Philip Marsh. His heart swelled with an engrossing wish to cancel, as far as he could, the great outrage he had committed on society by taking the life of one of its members. A great crime sometimes revolutionizes a character. For that purpose he would cheerfully have endured any pains or privations, however severe; and he rejoiced in all the additional risk he ran, for the preservation or recovery of those unhappy sufferers. It even seemed as if he were thus making interest in the Courts of Heaven. How many new comers to the immortal land must have passed its golden arches, with the thought of his devoted sympathy fresh within them. Who should say he was not already interceded for at the throne of God?

Late one evening Philip was walking slowly home, faint with the labors of the day, to gain that repose which would fit him for further efforts. His course led him through one of those thoroughfares that intersect the eastern part of Grand street; and in the solemn stillness of the time, his attention was arrested by the low sobbing of a child whose face could be indistinctly seen at an open basement window. Philip stepped closer, paused, and leaning down, saw that it was a young boy.

"Why are you crying, my little son?" said he.

The child ceased his sobs and looked up, but made no answer.

"Are you alone here?" continued Philip. "Is your father or mother sick?"

"My brother is sick," answered the child. "I have no father. He is dead."

"Did he die of the cholera, then?"

"No," replied the boy, "a bad man killed him a year ago."

Philip's heart quivered as if some harsh instrument had cut into it. A dim foreboding, not without joy, too, came dreamily to him.

"What is your name, my poor boy?" he asked.

"Adam Covert," said the child.

And at the same moment Philip was down the area steps, and had entered the door.

By the death of Covert, his two children were left without any protector, and almost without a shelter. The lawyer's business was conducted on a plan so entirely without method—the knowledge of its details being confined to himself almost exclusively—that it would have been difficult for anyone to realize the smallest sum over the demands against him. In this state of things several rapacious creditors came in, and took possession of all that remained.

The elder of the two young Coverts was a lad of about eighteen, an industrious and intelligent youngster, whose earnings now sufficed for the support of himself and his little brother. They rubbed along tolerably well, until the coming of the cholera, which broke up the boarding-house where they had made their home, dispersed the boarders, and drove off the frightened landlady and her family among some distant country relations. The orphans, too poor to go with the rest, obtained permission to occupy the basement of the house, and the elder continued his avocations for a while longer, when unfortunately his business stopped, and of course his wages with it.

The afternoon previous to Philip's accidental encounter with the child at the window, poor living and a disturbed mind had done their work on the unemployed lad, and he began to feel the symptoms of the prevailing illness. There was no aid, no friend, no doctor near. He went forth into the street, but feared that he might perhaps die there upon the public walk, and returned to his dwelling again, comforting his brother as well as he could.

And now, Philip, thanking the indulgence of God, which had vouchsafed him this happiness, was the nurse, the friend, and the physician of the sick youth. Hardly for a moment stirred he from the room. He always carried about him the medicines necessary in such cases, and here all his experience and skill were taxed to their utmost.

Heaven blessed those exertions, and the boy recovered his health again.

But this was Philip's crowning act of recompense. From the very hour when his young patient was beyond danger, the over-wearied man began to droop. His illness however was not long. He wrote a short note to his sister, who was many miles away at the house of a distant relative—bequeathed his property to the boys whom he had made fatherless—(after the death of Covert, the orphans of course received their inheritance at once)—and a few hours afterward, calmly passed Philip Marsh from the circuit of that life, which, young as he was, had been to him little else than a scene of crime, suffering and repentance.

Some of my readers may, perhaps, think that he ought to have been hung at the time of his crime. I must be pardoned if I think differently.

SOME FACT-ROMANCES.

AS far as the essential parts of the following little incidents are concerned, the reader has the pledged personal veracity of the writer—must it be said, not only as a writer, but as a man?—that they literally came to pass, as now told. They may not be considered so romantic as if they had merely an imaginary existence—for though fact is indeed stronger than fable, it is hardly ever realized to be so. Even while we are thrilled most deeply by the sight or hearing of a real death under affecting circumstances, we do not look upon it as equally sentimental with a death described in a novel, or seen upon the stage.

Still, truth has a great charm—and I would try it against romance, even on romance's chosen ground of love and death. Therefore have I rummaged over the garners of my observation and memory for the following anecdotes—and therefore I present them, with a determination to go not a bit beyond the limits of fact. POPE's lady friend was charmed with PLUTARCH, until she found that he was an authentic biographer—so called—and then she threw his works away. I have more confidence in the judgment of intelligent American women, and men too, than to think they can act after such a fashion.

I. On the Huntington south shore of LONG ISLAND, there is a creek, near the road called "GUNNETANG," and the mouth of this creek, emptying into the bay, is reported to be so deep that no lines have ever yet sounded its bottom. It sometimes goes by the name of "Drowning Creek," which was given to it by a circumstance which I will relate. It is a universal summer custom on LONG ISLAND to have what are called "beach-parties;" that is, collections of people, young and old, each bringing a lot of provisions and drink, and who sail over early in the morning to the beach, which breaks off the Atlantic waves from the island's "sea-girt shore," and spend the day there. Many years ago, such a party went over from GUNNETANG. The leader of the rest, and owner of the boat, was a young farmer of the neighborhood, a fellow full of life and fun, who, with many others, had his sweetheart and his sister on board. The day was fine, and they enjoyed the jaunt gloriously. They bathed in the surf, danced, told stories, ate and drank, amused themselves with music, plays, games, and so on, and ranged over the beach in search of the eggs of the sea-gull, who lays in no nest but the warm sand, exposed to the sun, which makes a first rate natural ecaliobeon. (I have sometimes gathered a hundred of these eggs on the sandbanks there in an hour; they are palatable, and half the size of hen's eggs.)

Towards the latter part of the afternoon, the party set out on their return, and made the greater haste, as a thunder-shower seemed to be gathering overhead. They had crossed the bay, and were just entering the mouth of the creek I have mentioned, when the storm burst, and a sudden flaw of wind capsized the boat. Most Long Islanders are good swimmers, and as the stream was but a few yards wide, the men supported the women and children to the banks. The young man, the owner of the boat, grasped his sister with one arm, and struck out for the shore with the other. When he was within a rod of it, he heard a slight exclamation from the upturned boat, and turning his head, he saw the girl he loved slip into the water. Yielding to a sudden impulse, he shook off his sister, swam back, dived, and clutching the sinking one by her hair and dress, brought her safely to the shore. He then again swam back for his sister, and for many long and dreadful minutes beat the dark waters, and dived—but beat and dived in vain. The girl drowned, and her body was never more seen.

From that time forth the young man's character was entirely changed. He laughed no more, and no more engaged in the country jollities. He married his sweetheart, but it was a cold and unfriendly union. About a year from this, he began to pine and droop strangely. He had no disease—at least none that is treated of in medical works—but his heart withered away, as it were. In dreams, the chill of his sister's dripping hair was against his cheek, and he would awake with a cry of pain. Moping and sinking thus, he gradually grew weaker and weaker, and at last died. The story is yet told among the people thereabouts; and often, when sailing out of the creek, have I looked on the spot where the poor girl sank, and the shore where the rescued one escaped.

II. Not long since, an aged black widow-woman occupied a basement—perhaps she still lives there—in one of the streets leading down from BROADWAY to the North river. She had employment from a number of families, who hired her at intervals to cook, nurse, and wash for them; and in this way she gained a very decent living. If I remember right, the old creature had no child, or any near relative; but was quite alone in the world, and lived when at home in the most solitary manner. Always she had her room and humble furniture as clean as a new glove, and was remarkable everywhere for her agreeable ways, and good humor—and all this at an age closely bordering on seventy. Opposite to the residence of this ancient female, was a row of stables for horses and public vehicles, doctors' gigs, and such like. At any hour of the day and evening, groups of hostlers and stable-boys were working or lounging about there—and the ears of the passer-by could hardly fail often to hear coarse oaths and indecent ribaldry. The old black woman, smoking her pipe of an evening at her door over the way, suffered considerable annoyance from this swearing and obscenity. She was a pious woman, not merely in profession but practice. For several weeks, at intervals, she had noticed a barefooted young girl, of twelve or thirteen years, strolling about, and frequently stopping at the stables. This girl was a deaf mute, the daughter of a wretched intemperate couple in the neighborhood, who were letting her grow up as the weeds grow.—With no care and guidance for her young steps, she had before her the darkest and dreariest of prospects. What, under such circumstances, could be expected of her future years but degradation, misery and crime? The old woman had many anxious thoughts about the little girl, and shuddered at the fate which seemed prepared for her. She at last resolved to make an effort in behalf of the hapless one. She had heard of the noble institutions provided for the deaf and dumb, and how the sealed avenues of the senses are almost opened to them again there. Upon making inquiry, she found that in the case of her young neighbor, the payment of a certain sum of money—two hundred dollars, I think it was—would be necessary, preparatory to her admission into a certain NEW-YORK institution. Whether any payment was required after this, I have forgotten, but the sum in advance was indispensable. The old woman had got quite well acquainted with the child, and discovered in her that quickness and acuteness for which her unfortunate kind are remarkable. She determined to save her—to turn her path aside from darkness to light. Day after day, then, and night after night, whenever her work would permit, went forth the old woman, with letters and papers, to beg subscriptions from the charitable, for that most holy object. Among the families where she was known, she always succeeded in getting something—sometimes half a dollar, sometimes two, and sometimes five and even ten dollars. But where she was a stranger, she rarely received any answer to her request, except a rude denial, or a contemptuous sneer. Most of them suspected her story to be a fabrication—although she had provided herself with incontestable proofs of its truth, which she always carried with her. For a long time, it seemed a hopeless effort, and yet she persevered—contributing from her own scanty means every cent that she could spare. Need I say that heaven blessed this poor creature's work—that she succeeded in getting the requisite sum, and that the girl was soon afterwards an inmate of the Asylum. Whether the aged widow still lives in her basement, and what has happened since in the life of the girl, I know not. But surely a purer or more elevated deed of disinterested love and kindness never was performed! In all that I have ever heard or read, I do not know a better refutation of those scowling dogmatists who resolve the cause of all the actions of mankind into a gross motive of pleasing the abstract self.

III. I became acquainted some seasons since with a gentleman who had emigrated from FRANCE, and then lived in a pleasant country town, about twenty miles from this metropolis. He was a mild, but somewhat eccentric person; and on the farm which he owned—for he possessed considerable wealth—everything was permitted to go to rack. Cattle strayed away, fences fell, hay was unmowed; and if the owner had not drawn a handsome income from funds in the city, everybody in his house might have starved to death. The people round about thought him deranged, which perhaps was sometimes not far from the truth. But he never offended or harmed anybody, and was therefore permitted to go his own way, without any one's interference. He had three children, all of them grown and away from home. The sons were employed in some mercantile establishment in NEW-YORK, in which city the daughter, who was married, also lived. The wife of the emigrant was a gentle-mannered and most lady-like woman, of a delicate appearance, and always looked to me like one in a hopeless consumption. The neighbors said she was never seen to smile. One day the gentleman set out for NEW-YORK, with the intention of procuring medical advice for his wife, who accompanied him. After arriving there, and consulting several physicians, he took a sudden notion, the second day afterwards, to return to his farm, and carry his wife with him. The physicians pronounced the lady's removal highly improper; but he made his preparations in half an hour, and without the knowledge of his children, started away. The wife, so weak that she could not sit upright, was carried in a kind of covered wagon, on a bed. They crossed the BROOKLYN ferry, and when out near BEDFORD, the gentleman gave the reins of the horses to a hired man who accompanied him, and declared his intention of going forward on foot. He did so. The hired man drove on a couple of miles, and then stopped a while, jumped on the ground, and lifted the covering of the wagon to see how the sick woman was getting on. She was a lifeless corpse! The man stood for a minute motionless with horror. He then drove the wagon aside from the middle of the road, unhitched both the horses, tied one to a tree, jumped on the back of the other, and rode rapidly forward to overtake the husband. Three hot weary miles ahead he came up to him. He told his story, and the other listened, but made no answer. The hired man impressed upon him the necessity of returning immediately, but he declined, and rushed wildly forward on the turnpike toward the town where he lived. Arrived there, he passed directly by his own door, without stopping, and went down to a swampy wood of considerable extent, that lies a couple of miles beyond the village. In that wood, he wandered about for three days and nights, and when found at the end of that time, all pale, ragged, weak and bloody, was a confirmed maniac. They sent him off to one of the Insane Retreats, where, if alive, he no doubt remains at this moment.

The hired man, when he came back to the corpse, carried it to the nearest house, and then returned to NEW-YORK, and gave information to the sons, who, of course, took measures to have the due ceremonies of burial immediately performed.

IV. SAUNDERS, that unhappy boy, now in the State's Prison for his forgeries on his employers, AUSTIN & WILMERDING, once boarded in the same house with me. Soon after his arrest, I visited the Centre-street "Tombs," and went into his cell to see him. He gave me a long account of the commission of the crime, and of his doings down to the time of his capture at BOSTON. It was all a disgusting story of villany and conceit. He was a flippant boy, whose head, I think, was turned by melo-dramas and the JACK SHEPPARD order of novels—all but one little item. When he had received the money, and every moment was worth diamonds to him—he intended to sail in the Great Western, it will be remembered—he spent an hour in going up to a pawnbroker's shop in the BOWERY, to get a little piece of jewellery he had in pledge there—a keepsake from his dead mother. He told me in his cell that he would have given a thousand dollars for another half hour, yet he could not go away without that locket. That half hour cost him the doom he afterwards had meted out to him.

V. When my mother was a girl, the house where she and her parents lived was in a gloomy wood, out of the way from any village or thick settlement. One morning in AUGUST, my grandfather had some business a number of miles from home, and putting a saddle on his favorite horse DANDY—a creature he loved next to his wife and children —he rode away to attend to it. When nightfall came, and my grandfather did not return, my grandmother began to feel a little uneasy. As the night advanced, she and her daughter sitting up impatient for the return of the absent husband and father, a terrible storm gathered, in the middle of which their ears joyed to hear the well-known clatter of DANDY's hoofs. My grandmother sprung to the door, but upon opening it, she almost fainted in my mother's arms. For there stood DANDY, saddled and bridled, but no signs of my grandfather. My mother stepped out, and found that the bridle was broken, and the saddle soaked with rain and covered with mud. Sick at heart, they returned into the house. It was now after midnight, and the storm had quite passed over. Then in the stillness of their dreary watching, they heard something in the next room—the "spare-room"—which redoubled their terror. They heard the slow heavy footfall of a man walking. Tramp! tramp! tramp! it went—

three times solemnly and deliberately, and then all was hushed again. By any, who, in the middle of the night, have had the chill of a vague unknown horror creep into their very souls, it can well be imagined how they passed the time now. My mother sprang to the door and turned the key, and spoke what words of cheer she could force through her lips to the ears of her terrified parent.

   The dark hours crept slowly on, and at last a little tinge of daylight was seen through the eastern windows. Almost simultaneously with it, a bluff voice was heard some distance off, and the plash of a horse galloping along the soft wet road. That bluff halloo came to the pallid and exhausted females, like a cheer from a passing ship to starving mariners on a wreck at sea. My grandmother opened the door this time to behold the red laughing face of her husband, and to hear him tell how, after the storm was over, and he went to look for DANDY, whom he had fastened under a shed, he discovered that the skittish creature had broken his bridle, and run away home—and how he could not get another horse for love or money at that hour of the night—and how he was fain forced to stop until nearly daylight. Then told my grandmother her story—her terror and her fears, and how she had heard heavy footfalls in the parlor—whereat my grandfather laughed, and walked to the door between the rooms, and unlocked it, and saw nothing but darkness, for the shutters were closed. My mother and grandmother followed timidly, though they now began to fear the discovery of some comical reason for their alarm. My grandfather threw open the shutters; and then they all swept their sight round the room—after which such a guffaw of laughter came from the husband's capacious mouth, that DANDY, away up in the barn-yard, sent back an answering neigh, in recognition.

   Three or four days previously, my mother had broken off from a peach tree in the garden, a branch uncommonly full of fruit, of a remarkable size and beauty. She brought it in, and placed it amid the flowers and other simple ornaments, on the high shelf over the parlor fire-place. The night before, while the mother and daughter were watching, three of the peaches, over-ripe, had dropped, one after another, on the floor, and my mother's and grandmother's terrified imaginations had converted the harmless fruit into human heels! There, then, was the mystery, and there lay the beautiful peaches—which my grandfather laughed at so convulsively, that my provoked grandame, after laughing a while too, picked them up, and half jokingly, half seriously, thrust them so far into the open jaws of her husband, that he was nigh to have been choked in good earnest.

———

THE SHADOW AND THE LIGHT OF A YOUNG MAN'S SOUL.

WHEN young Archibald Dean went from the city—(living out of which he had so often said was no living at all)—went down into the country to take charge of a little district school, he felt as though the last float-plank which buoyed him up on hope and happiness, was sinking, and he with it. But poverty is as stern, if not as sure, as death and taxes, which Franklin called the surest things of the modern age. And poverty compelled Archie Dean; for when the destructive New-York fire of '35 happened, ruining so many property owners and erewhile rich merchants, it ruined the insurance offices, which of course ruined those whose little wealth had been invested in their stock. Among hundreds and thousands of other hapless people, the aged, the husbandless, the orphan, and the invalid, the widow Dean lost every dollar on which she depended for subsistence in her waning life. It was not a very great deal; still it had yielded, and was supposed likely to yield, an income large enough for her support, and the bringing up of her two boys. But, when the first shock passed over, the cheerful-souled woman dashed aside, as much as she could, all gloomy thoughts, and determined to stem the waters of roaring fortune yet. What troubled her much, perhaps most, was the way of her son Archibald. "Unstable as water," even his youth was not a sufficient excuse for his want of energy and resolution; and she experienced many sad moments, in her maternal reflections, ending with the fear that he would "not excel." The young man had too much of that inferior sort of pride which fears to go forth in public with anything short of fashionable garments, and hat and boots fit for fashionable criticism. His cheeks would tingle with shame at being seen in any working capacity: his heart sunk within him, if his young friends met him when he showed signs of the necessity of labor, or of the absence of funds. Moreover, Archie looked on the dark side of his life entirely too often; he pined over his deficiencies, as he called them, by which he meant mental as well as pecuniary wants....... But to do the youth justice, his good qualities must be told, too. He was unflinchingly honest; he would have laid out a fortune, had he possessed one, for his mother's comfort; he was not indisposed to work, and work faithfully, could he do so in a sphere equal to his ambition; he had a benevolent, candid soul, and none of the darker vices which are so common among the young fellows of our great cities.

A good friend, in whose house she could be useful, furnished the widow with a gladly accepted shelter; and thither she also took her younger boy, the sickly, pale child, the light-haired little David, who looked thin enough to be blown all away by a good breeze. And happening accidentally to hear of a country district, where for poor pay and coarse fare, a school teacher was required, and finding on inquiry that Archie, who though little more than a boy himself, had a fine education, would fill the needs of the office, thither the young man was fain to betake him, sick at soul, and hardly restraining unmanly tears as his mother kissed his cheek, while he hugged his brother tightly, the next hour being to find him some miles on his journey. But it must be. Had he not ransacked every part of the city for employment as a clerk? And was he not quite ashamed to be any longer a burthen on other people for his support?

Toward the close of the first week of his employment, the entering upon which, with the feelings and circumstances of the beginning, it is not worthwhile to narrate, Archie wrote a long letter to his mother, (strange as it may seem to most men, she was also his confidential friend,) of which the following is part:

"——You may be tired of such outpourings of spleen, but my experience tells me that I shall feel better after writing them; and I am in that mood when sweet music would confer on me no pleasure. Pent up and cribbed here among a set of beings to whom grace and refinement are unknown, with no sunshine ahead, have I not reason to feel the gloom over me? Ah, poverty, what a devil thou art! How many high desires, how many aspirations after goodness and truth thou hast crushed under thy iron heel! What swelling hearts thou hast sent down to the silent house, after a long season of strife and bitterness! What talent, noble as that of great poets and philosophers, thou dost doom to pine in obscurity, or die in despair! Mother, my throat chokes, and my blood almost stops, when I see around me so many people who appear to be born into the world merely to eat and sleep, and run the same dull monotonous round—and think that I too must fall in this current, and live and die in vain!"

Poor youth, how many, like you, have looked on man and life in the same ungracious light! Has God's all-wise providence ordered things wrongly, then? Is there discord in the machinery which moves systems of worlds, and keeps them in their harmonious orbits? O, no: there is discord in your own heart; in that lies the darkness and the tangle. To the young man, with health and a vigilant spirit, there is shame in despondency.

Here we have a world, a thousand avenues to usefulness and to profit stretching in far distances around us. Is this the place for a failing soul? Is youth the time to yield, when the race is just begun?

But a changed spirit, the happy result of one particular incident, and of several trains of clearer thought, began to sway the soul of Archie Dean in the course of the summer: for it was at the beginning of spring that he commenced his labors and felt his severest deprivations. There is surely, too, a refreshing influence in open-air nature, and in natural scenery, with occasional leisure to enjoy it, which begets in a man's mind truer and heartier reflections, analyzes and balances his decisions, and clarifies them if they are wrong, so that he sees his mistakes—an influence that takes the edge off many a vapory pang, and neutralizes many a loss, which is most a loss in imagination. Whether this suggestion be warranted or not, there was no doubt that the discontented young teacher's spirits were eventually raised and sweetened by his country life, by his long walks over the hills, by his rides on horseback every Saturday, his morning rambles and his evening saunters; by his coarse living, even, and the untainted air and water, which seemed to make better blood in his veins. Gradually, too, he found something to admire in the character and customs of the unpolished country-folk; their sterling sense on most practical subjects, their hospitality, and their industry.

One day Archie happened to be made acquainted with the history of one of the peculiar characters of the neighborhood—an ancient, bony, yellow-faced maiden, whom he had frequently met, and who seemed to be on good terms with everybody; her form and face receiving a welcome, with all their contiguity and fadedness, wherever and whenever they appeared. In the girlhood of this long-born spinster, her father's large farm had been entirely lost and sold from him, to pay the debts incurred by his extravagance and dissipation. The consequent ruin to the family peace which followed, made a singularly deep impression on the girl's mind, and she resolved to get the whole farm back again. This determination came to form her life—the greater part of it—as much as her bodily limbs and veins. She was a shrewd creature; she worked hard; she received the small payment which is given to female labor; she persisted; night and day found her still at her tasks, which were of every imaginable description; long—long—long years passed; youth fled, (and it was said she had been quite handsome); many changes of ownership occurred in the farm itself; she confided her resolve all that time to no human being; she hoarded her gains; all other passions—love even, gave way to her one great resolve; she watched her opportunity, and eventually conquered her object! She not only cleared the farm, but was happy in furnishing her old father with a home there for years before his death. And when one comes to reflect on the disadvantages under which a woman labors, in the strife for gain, this will appear a remarkable, almost an incredible case. And then, again, when one thinks how surely, though ever so slowly and step by step, perseverance has overcome apparently insuperable difficulties, the fact—for the foregoing incident is a fact—may not appear so strange.

Archie felt the narrative of this old maid's doings as a rebuke—a sharp-pointed moral to himself and his infirmity of purpose. Moreover, the custom of his then way of life forced him into habits of more thorough activity; he had to help himself or go unhelped; he found a novel satisfaction in that highest kind of independence which consists in being able to do the offices of one's own comfort, and achieve resources and capacities "at home," whereof to place happiness beyond the reach of variable circumstances, or of the services of the hireling, or even of the uses of fortune. The change was not a sudden one: few great changes are. But his heart was awakened to his weakness; the seed was sown; Archie Dean felt that he could expand his nature by means of that very nature itself. Many times he flagged; but at each fretful falling back, he thought of the yellow-faced dame, and roused himself again..... Meantime, changes occurred in the mother's condition. Archie was called home to weep at the death-bed of little David. Even that helped work out the revolution in his whole make; he felt that on him rested the responsibility of making the widow's last years comfortable. "I shall give up my teacher's place," said he to his mother, "and come to live with you; we will have the same home, for it is best so." And so he did. And the weakness of the good youth's heart never got entirely the better of him afterward, but in the course of a season, was put to flight utterly. This second time he made employment. With an iron will he substituted action and cheerfulness for despondency and a fretful tongue. He met his fortunes as they came, face to face, and shirked no conflict. Indeed, he felt it glorious to vanquish obstacles. For his mother he furnished a peaceful, plentiful home; and from the hour of David's death, never did his tongue utter words other than kindness, or his lips, whatever annoyances or disappointments came, cease to offer their cheerfullest smile in her presence.

Ah, for how many the morose habit which Archie rooted out from his nature, becomes by long usage and indulgence rooted in, and spreads its bitterness over their existence, and darkens the peace of their families, and carries them through the spring and early summer of life with no inhalement of sweets, and no plucking of flowers!

———

FINIS

The first known appearances of the short stories:

Death in the School-Room. A Fact.
The United States Magazine and Democratic Review, August 1841

Wild Frank's Return
The United States Magazine and Democratic Review, November 1841

The Child's Champion
The New World, November 20, 1841

Bervance: or, Father and Son
The United States Magazine and Democratic Review, December 1841

The Tomb-Blossoms
The United States Magazine and Democratic Review, January 1842

The Last of the Sacred Army
The United States Magazine and Democratic Review, March 1842

The Child-Ghost; A Story of the Last Loyalist
The United States Magazine and Democratic Review, May 1842

Reuben's Last Wish
New York Washingtonian, May 21, 1842

A Legend of Life and Love
The United States Magazine and Democratic Review July 1842

The Angel of Tears
The United States Magazine and Democratic Review September 1842

The Reformed
The New York Sun, November 17, 1842

Lingave's Temptation
New-York Observer, November 26, 1842

The Madman
New York Washingtonian and Organ, January 28, 1843

The Love of the Four Students
The New Mirror, December 9, 1843

Eris; A Spirit Record
The Columbian Lady's and Gentleman's Magazine, March 1844

My Boys and Girls
The Rover, March 1844

The Fireman's Dream
New York Sunday Times, March 31, 1844

Dumb Kate. - An Early Death
The Columbian Lady's and Gentleman's Magazine May 1844

The Little Sleighers.
The Columbian Lady's and Gentleman's Magazine September 1844

The Child and the Profligate.
The Columbian Lady's and Gentleman's Magazine October 1844

Shirval: A Tale of Jerusalem.
The Aristidean. March 1845

Richard Parker's Widow.
The Aristidean, April 1845

The Boy-Lover.
The American Review: A Whig Journal, May 1845

The Death of Wind-Foot.
The American Review: A Whig Journal, June 1845

Revenge and Requital; A Tale of a Murderer Escaped
The United States Magazine and Democratic Review, July 1845

Some Fact-Romances
The Aristidean, December 1845

The Shadow and the Light of a Young Man's Soul
The Union Magazine of Literature and Art, June 1848

Also available from Cholla Needles:

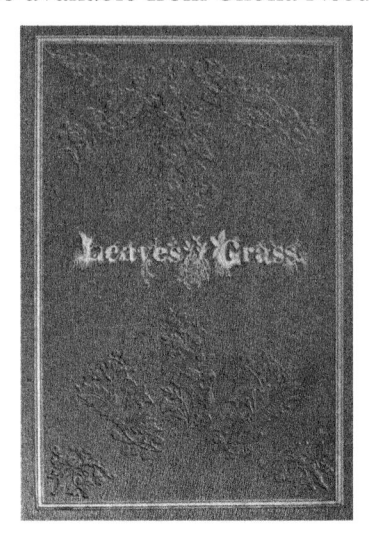

Leaves of Grass: 1855 By Walt Whitman
Reprint of original first edition, with original cover

period reviews:

"We find upon our table (and shall put into the fire) a thin octavo volume, handsomely printed and bound. We shall nor aid in extending the sale of this intensely vulgar, nay, absolutely beastly book, by telling our readers where it may be purchased." - Frank Leslie, *Illustrated Newspaper*

"In glancing rapidly over the 'Leaves of Grass' you are puzzled whether to set the author down as a madman or an opium eater; when you have studied them you recognize a poet of extraordinary vigor, nay even beauty of thought, beneath the most fantastic garments of diction." *The New York Daily News*

"We have glanced through this book with disgust and astonishment; - astonishment that anyone can be found who would dare to print such a farrago of rubbish." *Dublin Review*

Also available from Cholla Needles:

Drum-Taps: 1865 By Walt Whitman
Reprint of original first edition and sequel, with original cover

period reviews:

"In its way, it is quite as artificial as that of any other poet, while it is unspeakably inartistic...emitted in barbaric yawps, it is not more filling than Ossian or the east wind." - W.D. Howells, *Round Table*

"It has been a melancholy task to read this book; and it is a still more melancholy one to write about it... It exhibits the effort of an essentially prosaic mind to lift itself, by a prolonged muscular strain, into poetry...this volume is an offense against art." - Henry James, *Nation*

"...a poverty of thought, paraded forth with a hubbub of stray words..." - New York Times, *November 22, 1865*

"...inexpressibly pathetic..." - *New York Saturday Press*

Also available from Cholla Needles:

Three Novellas: 1842-1846 By Walt Whitman

A collection of Walt Whitman's three novellas never appeared as a single volume in his lifetime. We collected them together presented in chronological order for folks like us that are curious about the hard-to-find works of Whitman.

The first, and longest novella in this collection is Franklin Evans, which appeared as a short book on its own in 1842. Arrow Tip was published in The Aristidean, March 1845 taking a full 30 pages of the magazine. The magazine would usually run 10-12 page stories, and had published several of Whitman's short stories. This lets us know the esteem the editor had for Whitman's work. The last story, Fortunes of a Country Boy was actually serialized over twelve daily issues of The Brooklyn Daily Eagle and Kings County Democrat in 1846.

Whitman's overwhelming popularity as the Father of modern prose poetry, often causes his novellas to be overlooked by modern readers. You will enjoy this low-cost collection of seldom-read stories.

Also available from Cholla Needles:

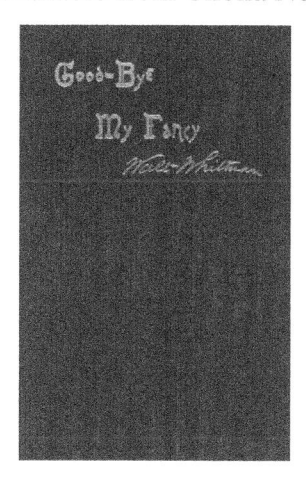

Goodbye My Fancy: 1888-1891 By Walt Whitman
Reprint of original first edition, with original cover

   This book contains the last two collections of poems by Whitman. They were placed at the end of the final version of *Leaves of Grass* (1892). Neither collection was listed in the contents, they were simply added as an afterthought. *Sands At Seventy* originally appeared in public nestled between two essays in *November Boughs* (1888). Three years later *Good-bye My Fancy* (1891) appeared as a small book. Whitman's essay, *A Backward Glance O'er Traveled Roads* is included.
   "With *Good-Bye My Fancy*, Walt Whitman has rounded out his life-work. This book is his last message, and of course a great deal will be said about it by critics all over the world, both in praise and dispraise; but probably nothing that the critics will say will be as interesting as this characteristic utterance upon the book by the poet himself. It is the subjective view as opposed to the objective views of the critics. Briefly, Whitman gives, as he puts it, 'a hint of the spinal marrow of the business,' not only of *Good-Bye My Fancy*, but also of the *Leaves of Grass*. After the critics 'have ciphered and ciphered out long,' they will probably have nothing better to say."
            - Published in *Lippincott's Magazine*, August, 1891

O Captain! my Captain!

O Captain! my Captain! our fearful trip is done,
The ship has weather'd every rack, the prize we sought is won,
The port is near, the bells I hear, the people all exulting,
While follow eyes the steady keel, the vessel grim and daring;
    But O heart! heart! heart!
      O the bleeding drops of red,
        Where on the deck my Captain lies,
          Fallen cold and dead.

O Captain! my Captain! rise up and hear the bells;
Rise up — for you the flag is flung — for you the bugle trills,
For you bouquets and ribbon'd wreaths — for you the shores a-crowding,
For you they call, the swaying mass, their eager faces turning;
    Here Captain! dear father!
      This arm beneath your head;
        It is some dream that on the deck
          You've fallen cold and dead.

My Captain does not answer, his lips are pale and still,
My father does not feel my arm, he has no pulse nor will,
The ship is anchor'd safe and sound, its voyage closed and done,
From fearful trip the victor ship comes in with object won;
    Exult, O shores, and ring O bells!
      But I with mournful tread
        Walk the deck my Captain lies,
          Fallen cold and dead.

Walt Whitman

Printed in Great Britain
by Amazon